DEATH IN WHITE SATIN

AN AL PENNYBACK MYSTERY

CHARLES RAY

North Potomac, MD

This book is a work of fiction. Names, descriptions, places, and incidents are products of the author's imagination, or are used fictionally. Any resemblance to actual events or persons, living or dead, is purely coincidental.

The reproduction or distribution, by any means, including electronic distribution, is expressly prohibited without the written consent of the copyright holder, except for fair use quotes in connection with reviews.

For information about this and other works of this author, contact the author at charlesray.author@yahoo.com.

Printed in the United States of America.

ISBN: 0615900461
ISBN-13 978-061900469 (Uhuru Press):

Death in White Satin

One

Rich people aren't like the rest of us.

They dress differently, eat different foods, and live in a different style from us normal people. It's as if they inhabit a parallel, but different universe. They live on such a high plane I don't think they even see us mere mortals, except when they need something from us. Like the gods on Mount Olympus, we're only occasional nuisances, to be ignored for the most part, and swept aside when we become to bothersome.

Try as I might, I simply cannot understand them.

My name is Al Pennyback. My full name on my birth certificate is Albert Einstein Pennyback, thanks to a mother who was enamored of the German scientist, and who dreamed that her only son might someday grow up to be like him. I disappointed her by joining the army right out of high school. My father, a

World War II veteran, was proud of me for enlisting, but he would never say so in my mother's presence.

Thanks to the chemicals in the water in East Texas where I was born, and the old-country cooking of a grandmother who only believed in boiling laundry, I developed an immunity to most of the illnesses that keep people from growing to their full potential, topping out at just over six feet, and now, at age 50, managing to keep my weight around two-ten with a lot of running, exercise, and meditation.

I have a rather easy-going view of life, inherited from my African and Native American ancestors, except where injustice is concerned. On that issue, the Scots who took dips in my family gene pool deposited the vast majority of my attitude; which is very Old Testament – the wicked should be punished for their misdeeds.

I'm a private investigator; have been since I retired from the army. I hung up my uniform after my wife Sarah and my son Ethan were killed when a truck driver ran a stop sign and T-boned the van Sarah was driving on Arlington Boulevard as she was bringing Ethan and some of his teammates home from a late soccer match. The driver suffered minor scratches. Everyone in the van died instantly.

I went into a funk afterwards, secluding myself in the little brownstone we were renting on the edge of Georgetown in the District of Columbia. I didn't shave or shower, and rarely moved from the sofa in the tiny living room until my friend Quincy Chang, partner in a D.C. law firm, talked me out of the house and into moving on with my life. After I officially retired – and, I passed on a retirement ceremony – he convinced me to apply for my PI license, and then talked his partners at Holcombe, Stein, and Chang into putting me on a ten thousand buck a month retainer doing odd investigative jobs for them.

It took a while, but I finally got over losing Sarah and Ethan. Sandra Winter, a teacher at Carter High School in one of the District's poorest neighborhoods, had a lot to do with that. I met her when I was investigating the shooting death of one of her students, at the kid's grandmother's request. We got off to a rocky start, and then found that we had a lot in common. She now spends the bulk of her time at my place, a converted farm house just off River Road in Maryland's Montgomery County west of Potomac Village. We use her little two-story house in Takoma Park in the District when we have to be late in the city.

You might wonder what all that has to do with rich people, and the answer is really very little. Other than the fact that I owe Quincy, and he'd asked me to take a case that I wouldn't normally take. I also had recently turned fifty, a temporal milestone that had put me off my stride until Sandra told me that I was just as capable and sexy at fifty as I'd been at forty-nine, and that I had to learn to accept change with a bit more equanimity.

Taking the case Quincy was proposing took all the equanimity I could muster.

We were sitting in Quincy's office on the eleventh floor of an ultra-modern building on K Street; me, Quincy, and the potential client.

Joseph Kellog appeared to be in his early forties, but with the bags under his eyes, he could have passed for ten years older. He had lank brown hair that flopped over his forehead and ears, and was wearing a pair of faded jeans, a slightly rumpled Washington Redskins sweater, and a pair of Nike sneakers that had seen better days. His nails, however, were immaculately manicured. In other words, he looked like a rich man who didn't give a damn what people thought about how he looked or dressed. He only did what pleased him.

I couldn't see at first glance that there was much of anything to like about him. Had it not been for Quincy, one of my oldest friends on an extremely short list of friends, arranged the meeting, I would never have agreed to even talk to him.

"Thanks for coming, Al," Quincy said. He rearranged the folders on his desk for the third time; clearly he was nervous about something.

"This is Joseph Kellog. His father, Jackson Kellog, is a client of ours. Joseph needs help that I think only you can provide."

"What kind of help?"

It was hard to imagine the son of one of the richest men in the eastern U.S. needing help that only I could provide. He could afford to buy whatever – or whoever - he needed.

Quincy knew how I felt about the privileged classes, which probably explained his nervousness.

"Maybe I should let him explain," he said.

Kellog looked at me as I imagine he would look at a butler or maid, just someone to do his bidding. He leaned forward in his chair, fixing me with a cold stare. Outside the window behind him, the slivers of cold blue sky that I could see between and among the skyscrapers of the K Street corridor, the home of most of Washington's high-powered lobbyists, looked less cold.

"Mr. Pennyback," he said. Surprisingly, his voice was soft and warm. "Mr. Chang tells me that you have a reputation for solving cases that the police have given up on."

I'm no different from anyone else. Like most humans, I respond to flattery.

"I've had a few successes," I said. "But, it's

primarily been due to paying attention to things the police miss."

"Well, I have such a situation. My fiancée was murdered recently. The police have arrested someone, but I don't think he's guilty. I'd like you to prove it."

It took me a few minutes to process what he'd said. Usually, people come to me asking for me to prove someone has done wrong.

"The police obviously had a reason for the arrest. Why do you think they're wrong?"

His face contorted into a look of befuddlement. He looked from me to Quincy. Quincy just shrugged.

"Well, like I just said," he spoke slowly as if talking to a small child. "The police have arrested the wrong man. I can't get them to listen to me. I've heard that you at least listen to people before dismissing them."

His tone said I was doing just the opposite, and I suppose I was. I reined in my distrust and mild dislike of people of his ilk. It doesn't pay to become like those you dislike, and when you're in business, it's never a good idea to piss off the people who pay your salary. Quincy, whose firm paid my salary, obviously wanted me to at least be nice to the guy. Since that costs nothing, and my middle class upbringing has taught me to always be polite, I softened my tone.

"Okay, good point," I said. "Why don't you give me some more details, though, so I know what I'm working with?"

Even as I said it, I knew it sounded a lot like I was taking his case. I had *not* decided yet to take his case. Quincy might have decided, but the final decision had to be mine. If the answer was no, I'd just have to find a polite way to say it.

"My fiancée, Penelope Laine, was staying with me at my parent's house in western Maryland. We were planning to get married next week, and my mother insisted we hold the ceremony there. Day before yesterday, someone stabbed her to death. The police arrested Luther Brand, our handyman, but I know he didn't do it. I can't get the police to listen to me. I'd like for you to look into it and prove Luther didn't do it."

The words tumbled out of him like water from a broken pitcher. He sounded serious. That left me with a problem – would I take the case. I needed to know more.

"Why are you so sure this Brand character didn't do it?"

"Because I know Luther, and he wouldn't do a thing like that."

"How do you know what he's capable of?" I asked this with a slight raise of the eyebrow.

The expression wasn't lost on him. He frowned.

"I just know," he said. "Luther is my friend. He knows how much I loved Penny. He'd never do anything to ruin my happiness."

Now, that pulled me up short. While he was talking, my mind was working. The information it pulled up was this: this joker was the son of Jackson Kellog, the richest man in the eastern U.S., only a shade less rich than Donald Trump. Kellog had made his fortune in plastics, getting into the industry before everything was made of plastic, and cornering many of the traditional markets, as well as carving out new ones. That he would be friends with a handyman was a little hard to swallow. I decided to call him on it.

"How is it that someone with your wealth comes to be friends with a mere handyman?"

"Luther saved my life," he said. Then, before I could ask for details, he began to spill his life story.

Two years earlier, he'd been addicted to cocaine and alcohol, and had been arrested after an altercation in a bar in Silver Spring, Maryland with a gram of coke in his possession. Despite his wealthy father's best efforts to keep him out of the slammer, he'd still had to spend six months in lock-up.

"Imagine if you will," he said. "A rich white

boy locked in the county jail with some of the worse thugs you could ever imagine. It was like feeding time at the zoo. But, Luther, for reasons I still don't understand, took me under his wing and kept the other inmates away from me."

"Was there a quid pro quo?" I asked.

His face flushed red.

"I know what you're thinking, but no, he just said he felt sorry for me. Anyway, when he finished his sentence; he was doing a two year stretch for assault and battery and drug possession, and got out a few days after I did, we ended up in the same drug rehabilitation program. I figured after what he did for me, helping him get work was the least I could do. It took some doing, but I talked my dad into hiring him as handyman."

"And, this was nearly two years ago?"

"More like eighteen months. Luther's been a good worker, and he's still a good friend. He knew Penny, and I can't believe he'd hurt her, much less kill her."

"How did he come to know her?" I asked. "Was she in the drug rehab program, too?"

"No! Penny didn't even drink anything stronger than an occasional glass of wine. Her roommate was in the program, and Penny used to pick her up after sessions. That's how we met. After I got out of the program, I asked her out, and the rest is, as they say, history. We fell in love, and she said yes when I asked her to marry me. Luther had met her a couple of times when she picked her friend Barbara up, and they got along. I just don't believe he'd hurt her."

"Why did the police zero in on him?"

"Because he has a police record, and he doesn't have an alibi for the time of the murder."

There had to be more than that, I felt, although the police are sometimes known for grabbing the most convenient credible suspect. Saves a lot of shoe leather, and makes the case closure statistics look good.

"Was there any evidence putting him at the scene of the murder?"

"Well, no," he said. "They didn't tell us much, but I got a sense there weren't any clues at the scene pointing to anyone."

I looked over at Quincy. A third-generation Chinese American, he can sometimes be hard to read. Now, though, he had a pleading look in his eyes. Like I said, he's an old and close friend, and friends do things for each other. He'd helped me when I was at rock bottom. He really, really wanted me to take this case, no doubt because it would please one of his firm's wealthiest clients. What the hell, I thought, it's extra money to go along with the ten grand a month retainer fee Holcombe, Stein and Chang, esquires, pay me.

"Okay, I'll agree to look into it, but I can't make any promises," I said. "If the cops with all their lab equipment couldn't find anything, there's little likelihood I'll be able to."

His face had been tense, but it now relaxed, and he smiled.

"I really can't ask for more than that, for Penny or for Luther," he said.

He almost sounded like a regular person. I reminded myself, though, that he wasn't a regular person.

"My fee is five hundred a day plus expenses."

I usually charge private clients a hundred to one-fifty, but with inflation, I'd recently raised my rates to two hundred. I figured, though, that a rich dude like this one should pay more than ordinary people. He didn't bat an eye. I should have asked for eight.

"Fair enough. Will you need an advance?"

"A thousand would be sufficient."

He pulled a thick leather wallet from his hip pocket and peeled ten bills from a wad of hundreds that would stick in a whale's throat, and passed them to me with a bland expression. A thousand bucks was to this guy just pocket change.

Like I said, the rich aren't like the rest of us.

"Is it possible for me to get a look at the crime scene?"

"Sure," he said, nodding. "Here are directions to our compound." He handed me a folded slip of paper from his pocket.

"You came prepared for me to accept the job, I note."

He smiled shyly and looked down at his scuffed sneakers. "Well, I was told that you tend to look out for the underdog," he said. "I know I probably don't qualify as an underdog in your book, but I was counting on you being willing to help poor Luther."

Two

It was hump day, and I'd gone to Quincy's before going to the office and checking in. Instead, I'd parked and walked back to the Waterfront Metro station and taken the subway to K Street. I knew Heather would be wondering, even though I'd told her where I was going. We usually did paperwork on Wednesday, if we didn't have an active case working, so we could end the week ahead of the game.

Heather is Heather Bunche. I hired her right after I started the company, and she'd just graduated from secretarial school. I needed someone to keep track of the paperwork, and she needed a job. Turned out she was also a whiz at pulling information from computers. It was a match made in heaven.

I walked east on K Street and then south on Twentieth to the Farragut West Metro Station. I took the Orange Line train to L'Enfant Plaza and changed to the Green Line to Waterfront, which is three blocks from my office just off Fourth Street in a two-story building that looks like an old roadside motel of the kind you see on back roads in the south.

The walk to my office from the Metro station was pleasant. There were only a few people on the streets, and the weather was warm for late October. A soft breeze was blowing in from the Washington Channel, bringing with it the smell of oily water and fish, which was an improvement over the usual sewer smell.

Heather, wearing a pink sweater, with her blonde hair tied in a ponytail, sat at her desk, sipping tea from a large mug and looking at some kind of graph on her computer screen. She turned as I came in. Her bright blue eyes sparkled in the light from the window as she regarded me over the rim of the mug. The smell of cinnamon filled the air.

"Hey, boss," she said in that little girl voice of hers. "I found that deadbeat you've been trying to track down."

The deadbeat she was referring to was a client of Holcombe, Stein and Chang who had run up nearly a hundred thousand in legal fees, and then skipped without paying. He'd vacated his expensive Watergate condo and attempted to make himself disappear, but Heather's skills at coaxing information from computers or from her network of secretarial and administrative assistant contacts in the area were hard to beat. I'd decided after ten years to make her a full partner, working with her to prepare her to get her PI license, and she'd taken to it like a cat to a room full of plump canaries.

"Where was he?"

"He'd moved up to Gaithersburg, and rented a cheap apartment there. Dummy used his credit card, though, to buy liquor at one of the county liquor stores. For a guy whose net worth is several million dollars, he wasn't too smart. He'd even put his phone in the new place in his real name."

That's another thing about rich people – well, a few other things. Most of them are cheapskates and misers, and a lot of them are relatively unintelligent. Oh hell, call it like it is; as my grandmother used to say, they're as dumb as dirt, and twice as nasty.

"I hope you handled it discretely."

She gave me a hurt look.

"Boss, I'm the soul of discretion," she said, pouting. "I called Quincy's secretary and told her. She'll know what to do."

And, she would. Just in case you think

CEOs run companies, think again. The most efficient companies are really run by the executive assistants, formerly known as private secretaries, who keep appointments on schedule, make sure papers go where they need to go, and know everyone and everything about the organization. Don't believe me? Make these people disappear for a day, and see how much actual work gets done.

"Okay," I said. "We have a new case, and I need you to work your magic to dig up some information for me."

I gave her the background, what there was of it, and asked her to get me as much information as she could about the people involved. She made a few cryptic notes on a steno pad, and then shooed me to my office so I wouldn't be in the way.

There wasn't much for me to do in my office. There's not much in my office to do anything with. I have a big executive desk that I got for a steal at an auction of excess office equipment, a leather chair, an extra chair that's wood with padded arm rests for guests, and a bookcase with a few phone books and atlases. The walls are bare except for two hunting prints and an autographed photograph of me with former Chairman of the Joint Chiefs of Staff, General Colin Powell, taken when I was a lieutenant colonel assigned to the Pentagon. On top of my desk are a telephone and a computer. The computer's one of the new laptops. I guess they call them that because they're small and light enough to fit on your lap, although I don't know why anyone would want to work that way. Heather bought it with some bonus money we'd received for a case. It was kind of neat. The keyboard and screen were compactly situated, and there were only two cables coming from it; one to the printer, and another to an outlet that looked like a phone connection, but was my connection to the Internet.

I checked my emails. Mostly junk. Spent a few minutes deleting them. Then, I switched to the games. My favorite is chess. I've been trying to beat the computer – vainly – for as long as we've had the damn things. Sometimes I think the machine is laughing at me.

I was working on my third losing game when the intercom buzzer on my phone rang. Another of Heather's innovations – we could talk back and forth without ever getting up from our desks.

"Yeah, what's up?"

My intercom procedure needs work.

"Got a preliminary data dump on your new clients," Heather said. "Want me to bring it in to you, or could I interest you in coming out here so I don't have to print it out?"

Okay; I'm no rocket scientist, but I'm no

dummy either. When she gives me those two choices, it's pretty clear which one she'd prefer I select. I broke the connection and went out to her desk. She smiled at me brightly. Sort of like the smile you give your kid the first time he uses the potty correctly.

She had her computer turned so that we both could view the screen, which was filled with text. As I looked closely, I saw that it was a series of bios on members of the Kellog family, starting with Jackson Kellog, the head of the clan. The information on the screen was in a document, which meant that Heather had found the information, copied it, and pasted it into a document which would go in our case file. She'd once explained copying and pasting to me, but I'd never really mastered it. Didn't I tell you she was a genius?

Jackson Kellog, age 78, was originally a native of Canton, Ohio, who had come to the DC area in his twenties to work as a clerk at the Washington Navy Yard. Mostly self-educated, he'd become interested in plastic fabrication, taught himself the basics, and started his own company making plastic gadgets for other industries. By the time he was thirty-five, he'd already made over fifty million dollars and the money just kept rolling in. He still maintained control over his company, but exercised that control from his mansion inside a gated and guarded compound in Washington County, Maryland, west of Hagerstown.

Mary Elizabeth Kellog, nee Byrne, age 70, was a Baltimore socialite, who dabbled in social responsibility by volunteering at a DC soup kitchen near the Navy Yard. She and Jackson met when he too volunteered to help out at the facility one day, and were married within a month. He was just starting his plastics company at the time, so they lived in his one bedroom apartment in southwest DC, much to the shock of her parents, who disowned her and refused to speak to or have contact with her until after Jackson made his first million.

Joseph Kellog, age 43, was their first born. They'd obviously waited until they were financially stable to start a family. Joseph had attended Johns Hopkins University in Baltimore, dropping out in his senior year. In line to replace his father at the helm of the company, he basically did nothing but attend parties, do drugs, and get blind stinking drunk. There was a string of arrests for possession, drunk and disorderly, and driving under the influence, but he'd only ever spent the six months in jail he told me about. His father's money and influence in the local community had saved his ass, and now he'd come to me.

Jennifer Kellog, age 30, was born when Jackson and his wife were in their forties. She'd been an honor student in high school and gone on to graduate from the Georgetown University with a degree in English Literature after dropping out of pre-med studies in her second semester. After graduation, she'd returned to her family compound where she lived with her parents. There was no indication in the records Heather unearthed that she'd ever held a job.

Heather, true to form, had gone beyond the family in her research, looking for information about the victim, Penelope Laine, and her alleged murderer, Luther Brand.

Penelope Laine had just turned 30 a few months before she was killed. A native of Washington, DC, she'd graduated from the University of Maryland with a degree in engineering, and had gone to work for Macy's in the District, first as a sales clerk in the jewelry department, and at the time she met Joseph she had been promoted to senior jewelry buyer for the Washington area stores. She had studied gem appraisal at her own expense, and so impressed the employers, they'd instantly moved her into the job and promoted her over more senior employees. Rather than inciting jealousy, however, her diligence and good humor, according to industry publication reports Heather had unearthed, her fellow buyers adored her. "She is just so giving," one was quoted in an article as saying. She lived with a roommate, Stella Clark, in a modest apartment in the Georgetown area. Since Clark didn't figure in the case, Heather hadn't bothered running a check on her.

Luther Brand was a 35-year-old DC native

who had grown up in Anacostia. His father had deserted his mother when he was three, and when he was five, she took up with another man. Brand's brushes with the law began when he was twelve, when he'd been arrested for assaulting his step-father with a baseball bat. He was let off when it was learned that he'd been defending his mother from the man's assaults. But, his troubles didn't end there. His mother died when he was fifteen, and he'd pretty much grown up on the streets after that, getting involved with the local street gangs. This led to a series of encounters with the system, with arrests for fighting, drug possession and use, petty theft, and assault. He'd met Joseph Kellog when he was near the end of his sentence for aggravated assault. He'd knifed another gang member who insulted him, putting the man in the hospital for two months. Everything Heather had found about him further painted a picture of a viable suspect in Penelope Laine's murder. The only thing he had going for him was Joseph Kellog's belief in his innocence.

It wasn't much to go on, but it was at least a start.

Now I needed to do some on-site research. It's one thing to read about people, but nothing beats locking eyeballs with them, seeing them on their home ground. That's part of what it's all about, this private detective business, getting out there and sniffing around.

I called the number Joseph Kellog had written on the directions to his family's compound. It was his direct cell line. When he answered, I told him I'd be visiting the compound to see the crime scene the following day. He responded well enough, but before he rang off, he cautioned me against bringing a firearm because of the stringent security rules at the compound.

He seemed relieved when I told him I didn't even own a gun.

Three

I knocked off work early and got home just a few minutes before Sandra pulled up in her little blue Honda. We had a light supper, listened to classical music on NPR for a couple of hours, and hit the sack early. She had early classes the next day, and I wanted to get an early start north to the Kellog estate.

At 6:00 a.m., I rolled out of bed. As I was pulling on my sweats, Sandra stretched and joined me. We went for a run in the woods behind the house, a nice steady jog of about four miles down toward the C&O Canal and back, downhill going, uphill coming back. Your thighs are burning after a run like that. We worked out the burn with a few minutes of kicking the crap out of the heavy bag.

It was a fine Thursday morning in October, with crisp air and the colors of fall painting the oaks, maples, and chestnuts, and the deer that were spooked by our sudden appearance in a clearing showing a bit of shagginess as their pelts prepared for the coming winter; the kind of morning when your breath is just a faint cloud of mist in front of your face.

Back at the house, I let Sandra shower first while I meditated. Then, after I'd showered and changed, we prepared breakfast together. Pancakes, pork sausage, hash browns, and scrambled eggs, washed down with grapefruit juice and freshly-brewed Colombian coffee from beans ground just before brewing.

We cleaned the kitchen, and then I let Sandra drive off first before I jumped into my green Volkswagen Beetle, a fiftieth-birthday present from Sandra, and headed out.

I drove down River Road to Falls Road, where I turned north to connect with I-270 north. It was a smooth ride as all the traffic was heading south at that time of morning; commuters from Germantown and Frederick heading to their jobs in Bethesda and the District. While I sped along at a comfortable sixty miles per hour, the southbound traffic was creeping along at about twenty.

It took me forty minutes to reach the outskirts of Frederick, where I ran into that city's rush-hour traffic, but in another ten minutes I reached the U.S. 40 exit and headed northwest. North of Frederick, the surroundings became more rural, with barns and agricultural supply warehouses dominating the landscape. When I turned west on Maryland Route 34, it was like I was in another state, or another world. Small frame houses with rusty cars in the front yards and rickety old barns, along with vast farms with large herds of cattle or acre upon acre of yellowing corn stalks lined both sides of the road, with the occasional expensive looking brick colonial sitting on a hill set back from the highway and accessed by a curving brick driveway. It was nothing like the brick colonials and mini-mansions of the areas around Washington.

The turnoff to the Kellog estate, southwest toward South Mountain, was a simple one-lane blacktop that cut through a stand of towering oaks that, like the trees behind my house, had taken on the red, yellow, and gold colors of fall, with little spattering of green leaves that clung stubbornly to the branches. The road curved gently from side to side, and the trees and brush grew almost up to the pavement. I started out at a smooth thirty-five until a twelve-point white tail buck suddenly appeared in the middle of the road ahead, like a statue, staring at my oncoming car. I stood on the brakes and came to a squealing stop.

The buck and I stared each other down for a full three minutes, and then he made a coughing sound, and a doe followed by two nearly mature fawns minced out of the trees and crossed the road. After they'd disappeared into the trees, the buck gave me another disdainful glare and then pranced off after them.

I did the rest of the three-mile journey at a sedate fifteen miles per hour. I've seen what a collision with a deer can do; the deer usually dies, but he gets his revenge from your having to replace your mangled front end. At today's prices, it's not chump change, and the car never drives the same afterwards.

I was concentrating so hard on avoiding having a deer draped across the front of my car, the gate across the road came up on me unawares. Had I not been driving as slow as I was, I might have actually skidded into it, which would have really pissed the broad-shouldered blond with the AR-15 across his chest that was standing in front of it, because I would have skidded across the spot he was standing on.

He wore a dull green uniform that stretched over shoulder, chest and thigh muscles, topped with a tan beret. The black leather portions of his canvas-sided combat boots were polished to a high gloss. The sandy-colored hair on the sides of his square head was cropped close; what the U.S. Marine Corps calls 'high and tight.'

In addition to the AR-15, he had a Glock 9 mm strapped to his waist, along with what looked like a stun gun, a flashlight, and a small portable radio.

Standing next to him, as still as if carved from rock, was the largest, meanest looking German shepherd I'd ever seen.

Man and dog regarded me stoically.

I eased the car to a stop about six feet from them. They didn't flinch.

Man and dog walked forward. He stopped just in front of the driver's side window and motioned for me to roll the glass down.

"You're Mr. Pennyback," he said. Not asked, but stated, like I'd damn well better be. "Please step out of the vehicle, sir, and open the hood and trunk."

His tone was polite, but there was no doubt that if I didn't get the hell out of the car, I'd either be told to turn around and leave – or worse. I glanced at the guard shack that sat just inside the gate, adjacent to the twelve-foot-high chain link fence that was topped with wicked looking razor wire, and which had a large dark wire intertwined with the razor wire that, from the ceramic connectors, was no doubt electrified, I saw a dark-haired twin of the man at my window. The second guard stood immobile, but even from a distance of ten feet, I could see that he was alert. No, if I didn't get out of the car, the option was 'worse.'

I popped the hood and trunk, and I got out.

Blondy quietly and efficiently went over every inch of the car. He had the dog sniff in the trunk, which in the classic Beetle is in front, and under the hood, which of course is in the rear. He took a small box of emergency flairs from the trunk.

"I'm sorry, sir," he said. "No explosives or flammables allowed inside. We'll hold these here and return them to you when you leave."

Couldn't think of any use for flares inside anyway, so I just nodded.

When he'd finished with the car, he took one of those wands they use to scan you in the airport and ran it over my body. Satisfied that I wasn't armed or wearing an explosive belt, he nodded to his partner. The large metal gate slid to the side with a whispering sound.

He gave me directions to the main house, and informed me that there would be someone there to show me where to park.

The drive, covered in sparkling white gravel, wound upwards and to the right. As I came to the top of a slight rise, the Kellog mansion came into view.

I don't know quite what I was expecting.

Maybe something that looked like one of those old English castles, complete with gargoyles and turrets. Or something like the Taj Mahal, which is becoming the in thing for the rich Indians and Pakistanis who are buying land along River Road just outside Potomac.

The Kellog place was a huge block, a massive tow-story white rectangle with a slate gray roof. Large white chimneys jutted up from the ends and center. Two porches rose from the ground floor to the second, on either side of a large canopied port cochere that went from ground to roof. The tops of the porches were rimmed in black iron railing. I could see another similar porch at the side of the building. Neatly trimmed shrubs nestled around the foundation, but none were placed where the view from the large triple windows would be obscured. Several antenna and two microwave dishes were perched on the roof at the right side. The lawn around the building was lush and well kept. It wasn't flashy, but it said, rich, rich, rich.

As I began the turn in the drive toward the port cochere, a large, broad-shouldered man, dressed in the green uniform of the security guards, and wearing a Glock at his hip, stepped out of the shadow and waved me to a paved rectangle off to the right. His head was bare. He wore the same Marine Corps style 'high and tight' hair as the guards, but his dark brown hair was flecked with strands of gray. His expression was neutral, but the way his eyes took in the Volkswagen, I decided he was all business. I followed his directions.

After parking, I got out of the car. He was already at my side. His face was sun darkened, except for the jagged white line of a scar that started in the center of his broad forehead and cut down across the end of his left eyebrow. He had cold blue eyes and thin lips.

"Welcome, colonel," he said. "We've been expecting you."

That brought me up short. I hadn't been called colonel in over a decade, except for a visit a few years back from an old friend from my Special Forces team, and I was curious as to how he knew. I looked at him with raised eyebrows.

"That shouldn't surprise an old Special Forces grunt like you, colonel," he said. "I'm in charge of security here. Of course, when Joe said he'd hired you, I checked you out. You were in command of a Green Beret strike team until a mission went wrong in Somalia. You quit and went to work in the Pentagon. When your wife and son were killed in an auto accident, you retired from the army and became a private detective. That's an impressive record you have. You been busy since, too."

Heather isn't the only one able to coax information from the ether, and like every other

American, my life's story resides in millions of bits of electronic data, there for the savvy researcher to pick over. The Kellogs were very security conscious. Made me wonder what kind of business old man Kellog was doing, but then, rich people are eccentric, and often have an over-inflated sense of themselves. Maybe it was a case of, he could afford it, why the hell not.

"Impressive bit of research," I said. "I guess that is your job. You have me at a disadvantage, though. Other than the fact that you're a former Marine, I know nothing about you."

I didn't need to go to a computer to tell that.

He touched a beefy hand to his hair. "I guess the haircut gives me away, but that's still impressive. Most people don't make the connection. Yeah, I was in Force Recon for twelve years. Rose to the rank of Master Gunnery Sergeant. Then, I decided my skills could make me more money on the outside. Name's Ted Wilson. I'm CEO of SecuroTech. We specialize in security for rich executives and others who are potential kidnap victims. Mr. Kellog, that's Jackson, is one of my top clients. In fact, he was our first client."

I stuck out a hand. "Please to meet you, Gunny."

His grip was strong and dry.

"You can just call me Turk," he said.

"Nobody's called me Gunny in years."

"I'm Al," I said.

He laughed. "With a name like Albert Einstein, I can understand that. What on earth were your parents thinking about?"

Damn, this guy was good. "I'll tell you about it over a beer someday."

"I can't wait to hear that. Say, is this a classic Beetle you're driving?"

"That it is. One of the last of its kind. Had a few mods, though, like a hood and trunk latch mounted under the dash, and I've upgraded the engine, but otherwise, it's like the original Beetle."

"Man, it's a beauty. I prefer pickups myself, but there's something about these little humpback monsters that attract the eye. Them Nazis might have been some bad fuckers, but they did know how to build a car."

He was referring to the fact that the Volkswagen, or 'People's Car', was first built in Germany in 1937, during the reign of Hitler and his Nazi thugs. Along with gassing and otherwise exterminating millions in their quest for the 'Final Solution,' the National Socialists gave us aspirin, high-performance optical lenses, and the progenitor of our Interstate highway system, the *autobahn.* You don't have to admire the inventor to like the invention, or vice versa; Alfred Nobel invented better ways to blow things and people up before establishing the coveted prize for peace that bears his name.

Just two old veterans gassing, but I had to remember that I was here on business. I was beginning to like the guy, though. Heck, he liked my car for one thing. Like me, like my car.

"I should get to work. What's the protocol for entering the house?"

"Nothing special," he said. "Joe'll be waiting for you inside and will show you around. I've got to get back to my patrol of the compound interior, and check on the patrols outside the fence." He pointed to the massive front door. "Just ring the bell. Mrs. Lee will show you to Joe's office."

He saluted and wheeling around, walked briskly away. I put him in his late forties, but the guy still had the bearing of a Marine. He also had some pretty serious muscle under his uniform. Probably worked heavy weights. I also had no doubt he was pretty good with the Glock. I reminded myself to question him later about the patrols. Not sure if it had any bearing on why Joseph Kellog had hired me, but I don't like leaving loose ends.

Four

A short, slightly stocky Asian woman, with lifeless brown eyes and jet black hair pulled back severely and done in a bun, wearing a black maid's uniform with a white starched collar and a white apron answered the door when I rang the bell.

She looked up at me from her five-two, and there was no welcome in her eyes. In fact, there seemed to be active dislike, but since we'd never met, I just assumed she disliked life in general.

"That Mr. Joe, he expect you," she said. Her voice was cold. "You follow me."

Without waiting for me to respond, she turned and walked off toward the right side of the building. We were in a large entrance foyer, and by large, I mean larger than most DC apartment buildings, beyond which I could see three stairwells, one in the center and one to either side, of a large room with a high ceiling with large crystal chandeliers suspended from it. I followed her, which wasn't hard. She had short calves, not as short as the Japanese, and stocky legs. That, and the broad forehead, pegged her as Korean. During my time in the army, I only visited Korea once, a temporary duty assignment to participate in an exercise. I didn't remember much about the place, other than the smell of night soil all over the country side, from the use of human feces to fertilize the rice paddies, the smell of the pungent *kimchi* that was often stronger and more offensive than the night soil, and the aggressive, hardworking nature of the Koreans, tough in a fight, and they seemed to fight a lot. I'd only been there a short while, but I didn't recall seeing them smile or laugh much except when they were soused from *makoli*, *soju*, or beer. The first two were potent concoctions made from rice. Beer, which they called *mekju*, was made from the same stuff we make it from, but somehow they made it a hell of a lot stronger.

We entered a long, wide corridor with doors on either side, and large Oriental vases spaced along the walls. She stopped at the second door on the right and rapped lightly.

"Yes," a muffled male voice said. "What is it?"

"That Mr. Pennyback, he here to see you," the woman said.

The door opened, and Joseph Kellog, dressed in green wool slacks and a beige shirt, stood there with a smile on his face.

"Ah, Mr. Pennyback, glad you made it," he said. "Thank you, Mary; that will be all."

The woman gave a derisive snort and glared at me before whirling around and walking away.

"Don't worry about her," Kellog said. "Her bark's worse than her bite. She never smiles, and I don't think she likes anyone."

"Yeah, I remember people like her the one time I deployed to Korea when I was in the army. Never mind that, though, I'd like to get some more details on your fiancée's murder, and see the crime scene if I could."

"Sure, come on in. I'll tell you what I know. I imagine you'll want to talk to the family?"

I nodded.

"Yes, but first, why don't you walk me through what happened that day."

He motioned me to a sofa that sat in the corner of an office the size of mine and Heather's put together. In another corner was a large wooden desk. Its surface was bare. Two large book cases, both empty, ran along the sides of the room.

"Would you care for something to drink? A cup of coffee perhaps?"

Again, I nodded, and he poured from a silver pot sitting on the ornate table in front of the sofa. The cup was fine china, the kind with the small handles that I hate because my fingers are just a bit too fat for them. The coffee, though, was exquisite.

"Okay, now about the day of the murder," I said, putting my cup on the table and leaning back.

It couldn't have been easy for him to recount the events, but he did a good job. The family, which included his father's younger sister, Abigail, and Penelope, had eaten supper, finishing around 6:00 p.m. Penelope had gone to her room after supper, saying she wanted to check the jewelry she'd be wearing for the ceremony, jewelry that included a five-carat diamond necklace that belonged to his mother, that she'd given to Penelope as a wedding present just before supper. In the interest of propriety, Penelope had been given a room separate from Joseph, though adjacent, but when she hadn't come to his room by 8:00, as she'd done every evening of the week she'd stayed at the estate, he went to look for her. He found her, sprawled in a chair in front of her dressing table, a large pool of blood on the floor beneath the chair, and the breast of her white satin wedding dress stained with blood.

He'd first checked for a pulse, but had known from her ashen skin that she was dead. He'd sounded the alarm and the police and ambulance had been called. I gave him points for coolness; not many people would think to check a pulse under such circumstances. Then again, he might have just been editing what happening for my benefit. I had a sense that Joseph Kellog hadn't had a lot of opportunities to demonstrate his manly abilities in his life.

The medical examiner had arrived with the ambulance, and declared Penelope Laine dead at the scene. The family had all been questioned by the state police homicide investigator, a Lieutenant Brian O'Malley. O'Malley then questioned the household staff, the Korean maid/cook, Monghee 'Mary' Lee, her husband Tongsu 'Thomas' Park, who worked as the compound gardener, and Luther Brand, the mechanic/handyman.

There had been no sign of any struggle, but the diamond necklace was missing.

The next morning, O'Malley returned to the compound and arrested Brand. His reasoning, according to Joseph, was Brand's prior record, a statement from the maid that he'd entered the kitchen to use the bathroom during the time frame congruent with the murder, and the fact that he couldn't account for his whereabouts between the hours of 6:00 and 8:00 p.m.

Joseph had used his father's influence to get Brand out on bail, on the condition that he not leave the compound. He was also required to wear a locator ankle bracelet that sounded an alarm if got more than a hundred yards away from his bungalow.

"I take it the police discounted the possibility of an intruder." I said.

"Yes, they did." He looked at me levelly. "With our security, and the electric fence, it would be impossible for anyone to breach the compound. In addition, we have roving patrols in the forest surrounding the compound. My father owns more than a thousand acres surrounding us, and trespassing is strictly prohibited."

"Hm, then someone inside the compound did it, clearly. Did anything unusual happen that day – before the murder, I mean?"

"No . . . well, there was one thing – Penny seemed a bit distracted during supper. It was as if she was worried about something. I asked her if everything was all right, but she just said her stomach was a bit upset."

"Were there any bad feelings between your fiancée and anyone else here; members of your family for instance?"

"No. Mom thought she was a princess, and Jennifer followed her around like a little puppy. I think my dad thought she might be a bit beneath us socially, but then, he thinks that of every woman I've ever dated. Aunt Abby, that's my dad's sister Abigail, is a bit batty, so I'm not sure what she thinks."

"Okay then, I'd like to talk with each of them, preferably one on one."

His face took on a worried frown.

"Uh, well, I'll see what I can do. My dad's something of a control freak. He might not like to have you talking to the others without his presence."

"In that case, I'll talk to him first," I said.

He looked skeptical, but nodded and scurried out of the room. He was back in a few minutes, now looking puzzled.

"He said he'd talk to you. His office is two doors down on the right."

He'd disappeared back inside his own office before I'd gone two steps. I stopped in front of the last door on the right. To my left was a glass double door that led out onto a side porch that was enclosed in large glass windows. I rapped on the door.

"It's not locked," a muffled voice said.

I entered. The office was the same size as Joseph Kellog's, but the desk was smaller, and piled high with thick folders, newspapers, and documents. A wooden rack containing a clear plastic letter opener sat in the center. Two large bookcases sat against the walls on either side. One contained a number of leather-bound books of different sizes. Books like I'd seen in library special collections – the expensive kind you can only touch with special permission from the librarian. The other was filled with plastic items. Plastic car, ship and airplane models, a full-size plastic football, and various medallions and plaques in testament to Kellog's pioneering work in the substance no doubt. On the floor beside the case was a full-size sword and shield in the transparent material on one side, and a set of crossed spears on the other. The man sitting behind the desk was slighter built and pale of complexion, but looked like a much older version of his son. His hair was thin and snow white, combed straight back. I could see liver spots in the thin hair at the edge of his hairline, and on the backs of his bony hands that rested on the desk. He motioned me to a straight back wooden chair placed centrally in front of the desk.

I recognized the technique. He was attempting to establish his dominance over me. I was pretty sure the seat was set up so that I'd be below his eye level; force to look up at, and to, him. Well, I was having none of that. I turned the chair around and straddled it, resting my arms on the back. His rheumy blue eyes regarded me narrowly at first, and then, he smiled.

"Well played, Mr. Pennyback," he said. He seemed impressed that I'd caught onto his little ploy and thwarted it. That probably didn't happen often. His voice was stronger than his appearance would lead you to believe. "So, you want to talk to me about Ms. Laine's murder, I take it. Surely, Joseph has told you everything we know about what happened – which is precious little, really."

Despite myself, I found myself warming to the old man. He played hard ball, but showed respect for those who could play in his league.

"I find that people's memories and perceptions often differ, even when they've viewed the same incident. By talking to each of you individually, I hope to get a clearer picture of what happened here."

He placed his gnarled hands together and balanced his chin on his fingertips, gazing at me for a long moment.

"I can't explain it, Mr. Pennyback, but for some reason I like you. Or, maybe it's that I respect you. You remind me a lot of a younger me. Okay, you talk to whoever you need to. I must say, I was shocked when the police blamed poor Luther, but they seemed so sure of themselves, and there don't seem to be any other viable suspects. I frankly had reservations when Joseph wanted to hire him, but he was insistent, and I guess we did owe him for protecting Joseph when he was in jail."

I didn't want to say that there were in fact several other viable suspects; namely, the members of the family; the other help. Money talks, though, and I doubt that the police, presented with someone like Luther Brand, looked too closely at anyone else. I work on the assumption that anyone near the scene of a crime is a potential suspect, and then I eliminate suspects one by one until only one is left. It's not rocket science, but it's worked for me. At the same time, I don't find it particularly useful to gratuitously alienate people I'm interviewing, so I didn't contradict him.

"Thanks," I said. "Can you tell me what happened the day of the murder? I'm interested in the time just before Ms. Laine left the dining room up until her body was discovered."

"There's not much to tell, really. It was just another normal supper."

"I understand she left before finishing her meal?"

"Well, yes as a matter of fact, she did. Now that you mention it, she did seem a bit distracted; sad even. I figured she and Joseph might have had a little lovers' spat. You know how these young people can be."

It was a bit disconcerting that he'd just assume I wasn't one of the *young* people. I was just getting adjusted to being fifty, but not yet at the point where I appreciated being including in the senior citizen population.

"Had she been this way before?" I asked.

"No, as a matter of fact, she'd been quite cheerful. My wife Mary Elizabeth gave her this necklace just before supper, and she was very happy. At supper, though, she seemed out of sorts."

"And, you have no idea why?"

"None at all. But, what does that have to do with her murder?"

"Probably nothing," I said. "I'm just trying to get a full picture. Now, she left the meal early; that left who in the dining room?"

"Me, my wife, my sister Abigail, Joseph, and Jennifer. Jennifer's our daughter."

"Who left next?"

His eyes screwed up in concentration.

"I can't really recall," he said. "I was talking to Joseph about plans for him to become more involved in the business. It might have been Abigail or Jennifer; I wasn't paying much attention. Mary Elizabeth, though, left just before Joseph and I did. She went upstairs to her room, and we came here to my office."

"Do you know where the other two women went?"

"I assume Abby went to her room; she tends to stay there except when she comes down for meals. Abby has problems sometimes dealing with people. When Joseph and I came here, I saw Jennifer sitting on the porch just outside."

"Did you see Luther Brand in the house at all during that period?"

"No. Luther rarely comes into the house. Oh, maybe the kitchen sometimes, when he's working on a car in the garage. He has his own cottage. Except for Joseph, he really doesn't interact with the rest of the people here at the compound."

"So, how, other than his police record, did the police decide to target him?"

"Oh that; Mary our housekeeper, that's Mrs. Lee, told them he'd come into the house around 7:00 and asked to use the bathroom near the kitchen. He does that sometimes, so she thought nothing of it at the time. She said she didn't see him leave. That was apparently enough for the police."

Not a smoking gun, but I guess I could see how the cops could come to that conclusion. It was just too pat, though. I wasn't prepared to accept it so readily.

I thanked the old man and asked where I could meet with the others. He arranged for them to meet me in the empty office between his and Joseph's. This room contained only a sofa and two wing-back chairs grouped around a large oval coffee table, a perfect place to chat with someone. The bookcases here contained what appeared to be leather-bound first edition books and little else.

Mary Elizabeth Kellog came down first, and the interview lasted all of five minutes. She recalled giving the necklace to Laine, recalled her looking sad and distracted at supper and leaving the table early, but little afterwards, because she went to her room, took a sleeping pill and had to be awakened when the police arrived. Talking to her was like talking to a department store mannequin.

"You say Ms. Laine was happy when you gave her the necklace?"

She looked down at her liver-spotted hands.

"Yes," she said. "She said it was the most beautiful piece of jewelry she'd ever seen, and she was a jewelry buyer, you know, so she should know."

"Yet, later, she seemed upset. Do you have any idea why? Your husband seems to think she and your son might have argued."

"I suppose that's possible, but Joseph seemed absolutely devoted to her. I didn't notice any tension between them at dinner. She just seemed distracted and sad, or maybe confused. She just picked at her food, and fingered the necklace. I have no idea what was bothering her, and, while I hesitate to contradict Jackson, I don't think it was because of an argument with Joseph."

"Was there any conflict with anyone else in the family, your daughter or husband, for instance?"

"Oh no, none at all; we all loved her. I think she was the best thing that could have ever happened to Joseph. He's spent so much of his life just drifting, I think she would have provided him with the stability he so badly needs. My husband can be a bit reserved at times, but I think he saw the same things in her that I did. As for Jennifer, she absolutely adored her. Penny was the big sister I think she's always wanted."

She seemed nervous throughout the interview, but when she spoke she made direct eye contact. She didn't know much, but she was being truthful about what she did know.

Jennifer Kellog came in after her mother left. She was a gangly woman with stringy ash blonde hair, an aquiline nose, and her father's broad forehead. She sniffled constantly as she talked, wiping at her nose every few minutes. She acknowledged that she'd left the dining room before her mother, father and brother, but claimed not to remember if it had been before or after her aunt. She'd gone out to the porch, she said, where she'd stayed until she heard her brother calling the police.

"You didn't see anyone else coming or going during that time?" I asked.

She wiped at her nose, and sniffed again. Her eyes didn't seem to want to focus on me.

"Well, I did see daddy and Joseph going into daddy's office, and later I saw Joseph leave; that was just before he found poor Penny: but no one else. Of course, from the porch, I could only see the hallway. If someone had gone upstairs, from the kitchen say, I wouldn't have seen them."

"What did you think of your brother's fiancée?"

She looked down at her hands. They fluttered on her knees, tapping idly. "Oh, she was nice, I guess," she said. "I didn't really get a chance to know her all that well. We only talked a time or two."

Funny that she had a different take on her relationship with the deceased than her mother did.

"Your mother seemed to think the two of you

were pretty close."

"Well, mother would," she said. "I guess we hit it off more or less. I mean, there's no one else my age around here to talk to."

"Did she get along with everyone else?"

"She spent most of her time with Joe. Mother liked her; hell, she gave her that expensive necklace that was given to her by her mother, didn't she? My dad, I suppose, liked her as much as he can like anyone. He's so totally occupied with his business, I don't think he really notices people."

"On the day she was killed, did she seem nervous, or upset at all?"

"Uh, no, not that I noticed. Oh, wait, yes, she did seem a little distracted at supper. I thought maybe she and Joseph might have had a little spat."

"A spat about what?"

She looked up at me, and then quickly looked away.

"I, uh, really wouldn't know. I'm just guessing. I can't think of anything else that she'd have to be upset about."

Whether she was withholding something, or just nervous at being questioned wasn't clear; she avoided eye contact, looking down at my shoes as she talked. She had something on her mind, but I sensed that pressing her would yield nothing. I decided to end the session, and maybe have another run at her later.

"Okay," I said. "Thanks for talking to me. I might want to ask you a few more questions later, and in the meantime, if you think of anything else, please give me a call."

I handed her one of my cards. She looked at it as if it was a scorpion, but finally took it and tucked it into the pocket of her blouse. When she realized that I wasn't going to ask her any more questions, she scurried out of the room as if it was on fire. I put her down as a nervous Nelly, in much the same category as her mother.

Abigail Kellog came in last. She'd been a beautiful woman at one time, but age hadn't treated her kindly. Her hands and arms were dotted with liver spots, and she had a little turkey wattle under her chin. Her blue eyes, though, were still bright and sparkling, which, after listening to her babble for three minutes, I decided didn't reflect what was going on in her mind.

She started off by flirting with me, and in mid-sentence changed to a long-winded tale about her life as a young debutante. I let her babble for a few minutes before holding up my hand to stop her.

"Don't you want to ask me anything else?" she asked in a querulous voice.

"No, that's all for now."

I thanked her and made my way to the front and let myself out. Wilson was waiting near my car.

"How'd it go?" he asked. "You learn anything useful?"

Five

"Nah, not much," I said. "I was wondering if you could show me around the property."

"Sure, what do you want to see?"

I wasn't sure, so I just said 'everything.' He walked me around the right side of the house to the large six-car garage, and on around the back – there were two porches on the back side as well - toward the small cottage where the gardener, Park, and his wife lived.

"What can you tell me about the family? Are there any simmering feuds or anything?"

"Feuds; no not really. Joe's not here all that much until lately, and I think sometimes he feels like the old man puts too much pressure on him about joining the business. Mrs. Kellog mostly stays to herself, and the old man's sister, Abigail is as nutty as a fruitcake. Jennifer, the daughter, is also something of a loner. What's any of this got to do with Miss Laine getting killed?"

"Hell, I don't know," I said. "I'm just trying to get a sense of this place and the people that inhabit it."

"I get it; doing recon."

I nodded.

As we approached the cottage, an Asian man, broad-shouldered and of medium height, came around the corner carrying a basket full of cut twigs. He looked our way, his expression unreadable. Then, he turned and went back the way he came.

"That was Park, the gardener," Wilson said. "He's married to the cook. They're Korean, and aren't very sociable. Been working for old man Kellog for more than twenty years I understand."

"What do you know about them?"

"Nothing, really. Like I said, they were working here when my company was hired."

Interesting, I thought, and something for Heather to look into. We walked on, past a large decorative hedge and around a turn, coming to another cottage, a copy of the first.

"This is where Brand lives," Wilson said. "He's probably inside. He hasn't come out much since he was let out on bail."

"I think I'd like to talk to him," I said. "I can make my own way back to the house."

He looked slightly miffed, or maybe disappointed, at being dismissed like that, but held his tongue. After a moment, he nodded and walked away. I approached the cottage door, which opened just as I was reaching up to knock.

Six

He was about five inches shorter than me, broad shoulders and overdeveloped biceps – probably from pressing weights during his time in jail – narrow waist, muscular thighs, and thick calves. The locater bracelet on his ankle looked stretched to its limits. His skin was the color of rich roasted coffee, several shades darker than my caramel complexion, and except for a puckered scar on the point of his chin, flawless. Dark brown hair in tight little curls clung to an oval head. His brow jutted over deep set brown eyes that bored into me. His fleshy lips curled downwards. He didn't look as if he ever smiled.

"What you want?" His voice was slightly high in a person of his bulk, and full of challenge. He was someone who'd spent much of his life challenging or being challenged, and the habits of the street never die, they just go dormant on occasion. In him, they were just below the surface, ready to bubble up at the slightest provocation, like someone saying hello in the wrong tone.

I introduced myself and explained why I was there.

His hostile expression softened maybe a degree or two. He stepped aside to let me enter.

I entered a small, neat living room. Inexpensive but tasteful furniture was neatly arranged giving the appearance of more space than was actually there. Several magazines and the latest *Washington Post* were stacked neatly on the blond wood coffee table.

I sat on the small chair to one side of the two-cushion sofa. He sat on the sofa, right in the middle on both cushions. Very territorial, he was saying that this was his and I was there on his sufferance.

"So, Joe done hired you to try and convince the cops I didn't off Penny, huh?"

"Something like that," I said. "By the way; did you kill her?"

He sat back, his lips curling down even more.

"Hell no, I didn't kill her. Penny and Joe the only people here give a damn 'bout me. The woman was my friend. 'Course, that don't make no difference to the cops. They got a brother on hand, they don't listen to a fuckin' thing, you know. Must be the brother did it. Ain't that always the way it is?"

"But, the maid places you in the house around the time of the murder. How do you explain that?"

He made a snorting sound.

"I was workin' on the old man's Rolls Royce; adjustin' the idle, and I had to piss bad. I didn't think I could make it back here, so I went to the kitchen and asked that Korean woman if I could use the toilet back there. Soon's I finished takin' a leak, I come back out here. I wouldn't be surprised, though, if that Korean bitch didn't say I stayed longer. She don't like me too much."

"She does seem the grumpy type, but why do you think she dislikes you?"

"I don't know. I think it she just don't like black people. She always snappin' at me and frownin' and jive shit like that. She like that old Korean man who used to run the High's near our apartment; always yellin' at us, and followin' us 'round the store when we went in to buy stuff. Hell man, you know them Koreans don't like us black folk."

I didn't want to go there. Relations between Washington's black and Korean communities had long been strained. The inability, or refusal, of the two sides to try and understand each other played a large role. When Koreans replaced Jews as the proprietors of most of the shops in the black neighborhoods, their lack of English and strange customs caused a number of incidents.

"Okay, you went in, used the toilet, and left. Other than the maid, did you see anyone else?"

"Well, when I was leavin', I saw Jennifer; that's Joe's sister; comin' down the stairs."

"What time was this?"

"I don't know. Maybe 7:00, or just before. I know it musta been close to supper, 'cause I was gettin' hungry."

"Did you see where she went?"

"Naw; I just saw her out of the corner of my eye. Didn't pay her much mind. She ain't exactly the type you do a lot of lookin' at, you dig."

"Okay, so you left the house. Where'd you go then?"

"I went back to the garage for a while, then I went home to make supper. I's there 'till the cops come knockin' on my door 'round 8:30 or 8:45.

While his expression as he spoke was hostile, he maintained steady eye contact with me. There was no sign that he was trying to be evasive.

"The cops didn't believe me, though," he continued. "Before I knew what was happenin', they slapped cuffs on me and accused me of killin' Penny. But, I swear 'fore God, I didn't do it."

I believed him.

"Okay," I said. "Joseph Kellog has hired me to try and prove that. I'm not sure what I can do, but I'll give it my best shot."

He looked surprised at first, and then his hostile expression softened.

"You the first one 'sides Joe what believe me. Why you willin' to take my side? Is it 'cause you black like me?"

"No, it's because I believe you're telling the truth. I'm curious about one thing, though; how did you come to make friends with Joseph? You two come from different backgrounds; I'd think you'd have nothing in common."

For the first time, he smiled.

"Yeah, you'd think that, wouldn't you? But, when they put him in the lockup with me, I guess I just felt sorry for him. That white boy in jail with some of the toughest dudes you ever seen; he was like fresh meat on the hoof. I guess it reminded me of myself first time I got locked up. He didn't have a clue how to survive, so I just stood up for him. If I hadn't, he'd of been killed the first night, if he'd been lucky. It for sure he'd been somebody's bitch."

Again, he came across as completely sincere. Sure, he was a tough, but deep down inside there was a soft core, and Joseph Kellog had tapped it.

"Okay," I said. "You just hang in, and I'll see what I can do."

I left him there looking bemused. I hoped I hadn't given him a false sense of hope. Proving his innocence wasn't going to be easy.

Seven

I retraced my steps back to the rear of the mansion. The Korean gardener was nowhere in sight.

Pushing open the door to the kitchen, I entered. The maid, Mary Lee, was standing at the sink, her back to me. She was washing a large aluminum pot. As the door clicked shut behind me, she whirled around, her almond-shaped eyes going wide.

"*Ohmana, Gamchagi,*" she said, almost dropping the pot. "You scare me. What you want?"

"Sorry to sneak up on you like that. I just need to see the guest room where Penelope Laine was killed. Can you direct me?"

She stood there for several seconds, her free hand at her breast, her mouth agape, glaring at me. Then, she pointed to a door to my right.

"You go through there. See stairs on left to go to guest room."

With that, she turned back to the sink and began scrubbing the pot again.

I pushed the door open and entered a narrow hallway. Ahead of me was a door, and another door was on my right at the end. I assumed the door to the right led out to the entry area as it didn't have a knob or lock. Pushing it open, I found myself facing the far wall, with the curved stairwell to the next level, and the large staircase in the center that soared up to a bridge that looked quite wide, with ornate railings spanning out from the stairs. To the right was an arched opening, through which I could see one end of a dining table with high back chairs, and to my left was the companion curved staircase.

I went up those stairs and found myself in a passageway that had a railing on the entryway side and a wall bisected by another passage on the other. Remembering that Joseph had said the guest room was over his office, I turned right and then left down the bisecting passage.

There were two doors in that hallway, across from each other. I opened the door on the left and entered a suite that would have cost $500 a night in the Ritz-Carlton Hotel. There was a small entrance foyer, leading into a large sitting room furnished in Colonial style, with oil paintings of flowers and landscapes on the walls. Beyond was the door to the bedroom, and to the right the door to the bath.

Penelope Laine had been found sprawled on the sofa, obviously not the one currently in the room, because this one showed no signs of having been soaked in blood. The door had been closed when Joseph came to check on her. Her assailant had had the presence of mind to do that before leaving.

I stood there, taking in the room, trying to picture what might have happened.

Laine's body had been found on the sofa, with no sign of any kind of struggle. This indicated that she knew her murderer, and trusted him or her (and, I wasn't discounting that one of the women in the house might have done it) enough to allow herself to be approached close enough to be stabbed to death. That didn't really let Luther Brand off the hook. By his own admission, the two of them were friends, so he would have been able to approach her.

The sitting room wasn't telling me anything. I went on through to the bedroom.

Her personal things hadn't yet been removed. Clothing still hanging in the closet, and her cosmetics still on the dressing table, along with a small leather case. I opened the case. There were several small pieces of jewelry, a couple of which looked expensive. Yet, according to Joseph, the necklace his mother had given her, which she'd been wearing at supper, was missing. That didn't smell like robbery to me. I made a note to check and see if she'd been wearing any other jewelry, and what had happened to it.

It was approaching noon, and my stomach was growling, but I had no desire to break bread with the Kellogs. I decided, instead, to drive to Hagerstown, grab a bite at a burger joint, and pay a call on the cop investigating the case.

Before leaving the room, I walked to the door that led from the bedroom to the balcony, which was the roof of the porch on the left front side of the building.

From the balcony, I could see all the way to the front gate, and the road which disappeared as it curved around a stand of tall hardwoods. I could see the forest stretching into the distance to the west and northwest, and that brush and trees were cut back from the fence creating a one-hundred-yard clear zone. At the corner of the fence to the left front, I saw a floodlight housing. This place had better security than Fort Knox. Of course, old man Kellog was probably worth as much as Fort Knox, too.

I heard a scraping sound below me. Looking down, I saw Wilson, the guard boss, standing under the porte cochere with Jennifer Kellog. He had his left hand on her shoulder and held her left hand with his right. She was leaning in close to him, almost resting her head on his shoulder. He looked around, but fortunately, not up, and quickly removed his hand from her shoulder. Reaching into his shirt pocket, he removed a small packet, and handed it to her. She put it in the pocket of the skirt she wore. I only got a glimpse, but it looked like a plastic baggy. Once more, Wilson patted her shoulder, and turning away strode briskly toward the gate. She looked to the right, seemed startled, and the quickly went back into the house. Shortly, the Korean gardener came into view from the right, carrying a shrub and shovel. He stopped and stared at the door. Then he shook his head and moved on past the front door, along the wall beneath where I stood, and disappeared around the corner.

Not sure what I'd just seen, I filed the incident away. My growling stomach was a higher priority at that moment.

Eight

I didn't see Wilson as I drove off the compound. The young guards at the gate, a different pair, saluted me as I drove past. From what I could see, Wilson ran a tight, military-like operation, but I'd expect no less from a former Marine.

I took route 34 east to Alternate U.S. 40 and then north to Hagerstown. It was fifteen miles to the outskirts of the town. I stopped at a Burger King just outside town and wolfed down a double Whopper with fries and a Fanta. My stomach's growls changed to purrs of pleasure after the third bite.

Sated, I asked directions to the county sheriff's office. It was northwest, near I-81, on Western Maryland Parkway, a large compound of buildings surrounded by a huge parking lot. As usual, visitors' parking was a marathon walk from the building.

In the lobby of the main building, I gave a bored looking young sheriff's deputy the name of the cop in charge of the investigation, Lieutenant Brian O'Malley. He took a look at my ID, made some notes in a large book at his elbow, and told me to have a seat on a plastic chair against the wall.

I sat there for ten minutes, watching the ebb and flow of humanity, some in shackles through the area. No one paid me any attention. I didn't let it bother me; I'd been here before – well, not here as in Hagerstown; I'd never even driven through the town before – but stuck in the lobby of a police station waiting for some overworked cop to clear whatever he was working on from his desk so he could come and try to persuade me not to stick my private nose in police business.

I must have dozed off from the burger, because the next thing I knew, there was a large object blocking the light. I opened my eyes to see a large body standing over me.

"I'm Brian O'Malley," he said without preamble. "You wanted to talk to me?"

He didn't come across as unfriendly; but, he wasn't exactly the Welcome Wagon either. I showed him my ID, which he glanced at, but didn't react to.

"Joseph Kellog hired me to prove his friend didn't kill Penelope Laine," I said. Two can play at the bluntness game. "If you don't mind, I'd like to talk to you about the case."

He gave me a sour look.

"It's not department policy to discuss cases with outsiders," he said.

"Look, I know there are things you can't tell me, but since I'm going to be working on it anyway, if we share what we can, it'll keep us from stepping on each other's toes."

"I can easily keep you off my toes, Mr. Pennyback. All I have to do is arrest you for obstruction. How's that sound?"

This guy was a hard case if I've ever seen one. Being polite and cooperative wasn't the way to go with him.

"I've been hired by a member of the Kellog family." That got a raised eyebrow. "They're represented by the law firm of Holcombe, Stein and Chang, and I happen to also work for said firm. If you do arrest me, I assure you, you'll be in court for the rest of your career."

That hit home. He paled, but his frown deepened. Whether it was the Kellog name or Quincy's law firm, I didn't know, and I didn't care. Whatever works is fine with me.

"Are you threatening me, Mr. Pennyback?"

"Not unless you're threatening to arrest me. Are you?

That got a puzzled look.

"Look, let's go back to the beginning," I said. "We got off to a bad start. I don't normally get in the way of police investigations. If you want to check me out, I can give you names in the DC Metro Police and the Montgomery County Sheriff's Office who've worked with me before. If in my investigation, I pick up leads that help you make your case, you can be sure I'll share them. All I ask in return are answers to a few questions, none of which should jeopardize your case."

He took a deep breath, and his expression became less stony.

"Okay, I'll give you a few minutes."

He walked over to the desk and spoke to the cop. He came back with a visitor's badge which he tossed to me.

"Keep it on at all times within the building, and turn it in to the desk when you leave. Come with me."

He turned and walked toward the stairwell. I followed.

Up the stairs, into a long hallway that ended in a large bull pen in which several harassed-looking men and women were either muttering into phones, pecking away at computer terminals, or questioning recalcitrant perps. His desk was in the corner near a window, indicating that he was probably one of the senior cops there, but not senior enough to merit an office with walls and a door.

He motioned me to the chair beside his desk. The desk was littered with folders and papers.

"Okay," he said, after we were both seated. "What do you have for me, and what do you want to know?"

I told him who I'd talked to, what I'd done, and what I'd learned, which wasn't much.

"I'm having trouble seeing Luther Brand as the perp," I said. "What was his motive?"

"Hell," he said. "That's easy. She was wearing a necklace with a five-carat round cut diamond worth roughly a hundred-fifty thousand. It was missing."

"I assume you searched his quarters?"

That brought him up short.

"Yes, we did, and it wasn't there. But, that just means he probably hid it somewhere. That's a big compound, you know."

"Did the victim have any other jewelry? Rings, earrings; things like that?"

"Sure, why?"

"Were any of them missing?"

"Uh, no," he said. "She was still wearing them. The necklace was the only thing missing."

"Does that make sense to you? If his motive was robbery, why not take everything? I found cash and jewelry in her bag as well. Wouldn't it make sense for a burglar to take that?"

He rubbed his chin.

"Well, I . . . I mean . . . hell, how am I supposed to know what goes through a perp's mind? Maybe he heard somebody coming and it scared him off. I don't know. Look, the guy's got a record, and it includes petty theft and assault with a knife. And, he couldn't account for his whereabouts during the time frame of the murder."

"Understand, but it still makes no sense. In addition, if he was scared off by someone coming, he would have been seen. There's only two ways out of that room; down a hallway to a stairwell which is in plain view, or over the balcony railing, and if he'd done that, he would have been seen by the guards."

He shook his head, and played with one of the folders on the desk.

"Okay, okay, I'll grant you that," he said. "But, if he didn't do it, who did?"

That, of course, was the question.

"If I knew that, I'd be giving you the name already. I'll keep snooping around, and let you know what I find out. Is there anyone else you think I could talk to who might be able to shed any light on this?"

"Well, there's the crime scene tech, she might have something you could use." He didn't sound as if he believed that. "And, you'll want to talk to the ME. Maybe understanding the way she was killed might help. Other than that, there's nothing I can really tell you."

"There is one other question," I said. "I assume you did a thorough search of the grounds. Did you find anything, the necklace, or a weapon?"

"We went over the place with a metal detector, but came up dry. Tell you the truth, the absence of the necklace or a weapon bothers me, but the circumstantial evidence against Mr. Brand is still pretty strong until someone better comes along."

He'd gone from hostile to amazingly cooperative in the blink of an eye. He gave me the names of the two people and directions to their offices within the complex, and even called them to let them know I'd be dropping in.

Dr. Leonard Scott, the county medical examiner, was an elderly, gray-haired man whose office was on the ground floor near the back of the building. I found him hunched over his desk, filling out a form. When I entered, he waved me to a chair beside the desk.

"Be with you in a minute," he said. "Have to complete this damn thing before I forget what I was planning to write on it."

I sat patiently while he slowly and laboriously filled in the tiny blanks on the form. Contrary to the myth that doctors have lousy handwriting, he wrote in a precise script. When he'd finished, he pushed his horn-rimmed spectacles up on his nose and looked at me.

"You must be the guy O'Malley said would be dropping in. You want to know about the Laine case, right? Not much to tell really. She was stabbed in the chest with some kind of really sharp, double-edged blade weapon. It didn't hit any bone, and left no trace fragments, and it's difficult to determine the length of the blade. I'd estimate its width, though, to be about one inch, although that's just a guess because skin tends to expand and contract making it difficult to determine blade size from the size of the wound."

This guy wasted no time, and thankfully, he didn't deluge me with a lot of medical jargon.

"So, she died from the stab wound?"

"No, not really. She probably went into shock when the blade penetrated, but it nicked the aorta causing exsanguination. She died from massive loss of blood."

"Would she have died quickly?"

"Son, the human body only has about five liters of blood. The nick in her aorta was pretty wide, and even in shock, her heart would have been pumping pretty fast. A person can bleed out in a matter of seconds if a major artery is cut. In her case, I'd say two to three minutes at most, but most probably much quicker."

"Have you identified the weapon?"

"No, I haven't; I just told you that," he said. "If it had hit a bone, there might have been residue that would aid in identification, but it only cut tissue, muscle, and the aorta, and there wasn't a trace of residue in any of that. Unlike the movies, it's hard to identify a weapon from the wound alone if there's no residue. I can't even tell you the shape other than it had to be double-bladed. That was obvious from the configuration of the wound, sharp at both ends. A single-blade would have only been sharp on one end of the entry wound."

I couldn't think of any other questions to ask him. He'd confirmed, though, my thought that the Kellogs had wasted no time cleaning the scene. I wondered, though, how the assailant, who would undoubtedly have gotten bloody in the process, could have passed through the mansion without someone noticing.

I thanked Scott for his time, and asked directions to the office of the crime scene investigator. Turned out, she was only a few doors away from the good doctor's office.

Lieutenant Susan Dickey wasn't what I expected. I'm not even sure what I expected, but it wasn't five-four, with bright green eyes, and red hair cut in a page boy, dressed in a blue jump suit that bulged in all the right places.

"Come on in," she said in a youthful voice. "Brian said you'd be dropping by. You want to talk about the Penelope Laine murder, right?"

"Yes," I said. "I know you guys arrested a suspect, but Joseph Kellog doesn't think he did it, and he hired me to do a parallel investigation. So, anything you can share with me would help."

"Brian said you might undercut our case; that true? Are you trying to make us look bad or something?."

"Look, like I told him, if I find anything useful to the case, I'll share it. If it turns out you arrested the wrong man, it would be to your benefit, wouldn't it? I mean, we're all after the same thing here – the truth."

She laughed. A musical sound. And, her green eyes twinkled.

"He also said you made sense, and weren't the type to be cowed by the authority of our badges; whatever the hell that means. What do you want to know?"

She motioned to a chair next to her desk. Her desk was small which meant that sitting in the chair, I was sitting close to her. She smelled like lilacs. I mentally slapped myself to get my mind back on business.

"The doctor said her aorta was cut; actually, he said nicked; wouldn't that cause a spray of blood, and get blood on her assailant?"

"It would if there were multiple stab wounds," she said. "In this case, though, there was only one stab wound, and if the knife, or whatever it was, was held in the wound, it might keep blood from spraying if it had any kind of hilt. Some would anyway, and the assailant's hand would get blood on it, but you wouldn't have the fountain of blood like you see in the movies."

"You think that's what happened?"

"Based on the way the blood was just pooled around the body, with no spatter anywhere else in the room, yes."

"Is that normal in a stabbing; just one thrust?"

"I haven't done that many, but those I have done have taught me that there's no such thing as a typical stabbing. Sometimes, if the assailant is angry enough, the victim will be stabbed dozens of times. Other times a single stab or a slash. This one was a single stab."

"So, does that tell you anything about the killer?"

She looked at me, her luscious red lips turned up in a half smile.

"Not a damn thing; well, one thing, and this is just my theory; the son of a bitch that did this probably knows anatomy well. The wound was almost directly over the heart. Probably the victim moved at the last minute, otherwise the blade would have punctured the heart."

"What about the robbery theory?" I asked. "I know the necklace was missing, but O'Malley said she was still wearing a ring and earrings, and I found jewelry in her bag. Does that seem typical of a robbery to you?"

"Actually, it doesn't, but like stabbings, is there really any such thing as a *normal* robbery?"

"Actually, there is. Thieves tend to fall into habitual behavior. It takes something really out of synch to cause them to break pattern. This doesn't strike me as a straight up robbery. So, if it wasn't a straight-up robbery, what do you think happened?"

"Be damned if I know, but I only get paid to assess what I find at the scene. It's up to the detectives to find the perp, and O'Malley seemed pretty certain it was this Luther Brand character."

"Do you think it was him?"

She laid her hand on mine. Her hand was soft, dry, and warm. She let it rest there for a moment, smiling at me.

"It doesn't matter what I think, but I get the feeling you don't think he did it. For what it's worth, I think you might be right, but if you repeat that to anyone here, I'll deny it."

"I wouldn't think of it. I don't make a habit of getting people in trouble if I can avoid it. I take it you and Detective O'Malley don't see eye to eye."

She batted her lashes at me. The room was getting uncomfortably warm.

"Oh, he's okay. He just has a blind spot about women cops and technicians, and he doesn't like to be disagreed with. I'm glad you're not the type to get people into trouble . . . although, I can think of some trouble it might be fun to get into with you."

I got it, and knew it was time for me to get out of her office before I found myself in a corner that would be hard to get out of. When a woman is making a pass at me, I think of Sandra and my unspoken promise to her, and try to find a way to disengage without insulting her. I patted her hand and gave her my best thousand-watt smile.

"Sounds interesting," I said. "Maybe when this case is done, we can discuss that."

Her smile got wider, and two spots of crimson appeared on her cheeks.

"I look forward to that."

She would hate me afterwards. But, I had no intention of ever entering Hagerstown again if I could avoid it.

Nine

I felt I'd gotten everything I could from the Washington County cops, so I turned in the visitor's badge and headed back to Washington. Luck was with me again, most of the traffic was headed north. I pulled into the parking lot at my office at a quarter to four.

Heather hadn't found any new information, but I had some more names for her to check. Ted Wilson, the security chief, headed the list, but I also wanted to know more about Tongsu Park and Monghee Lee, the Korean couple. As an afterthought, I asked her to check Abigail Kellog as well. I didn't think the batty old lady was the killer, but it pays to be thorough.

At five, I shut my computer down, told Heather to turn hers off and go home, and headed toward the farm.

I got the farm for a steal in an estate sale. When the old man who owned it died, his sons, who were living in California at the time, were more than happy to sell it so they wouldn't be saddled with the property taxes. I'd left the exterior pretty much unchanged, but the kitchen had been completely remodeled with all the latest gadgets, and I'd installed heavier doors and window alarms. After two break-ins; one when a couple of rednecks snatched me from my own kitchen, and the second when a Chinese gangster and his thugs came to kill me; I decided the cost was worth the peace of mind.

Sandra was already home when I arrived. As a schoolteacher, her hours are even more unpredictable than mine. Sometimes, she's home by four, other days, when the school has after-hours activity, she doesn't make it home until after nine.

She was sitting on the sofa with her bare feet up on the coffee table, listening to classical music on the radio.

"You look like you could use an evening on the town," I said.

"Actually, after the day I've had, I could use a good hot meal, a hot shower, and a nice massage." She sighed and batted her blue eyes at me.

I didn't feel like cooking.

"I'll make you a deal," I said. "I'll take you to a nice Korean restaurant, fill your tummy, then I'll bring you back here, and I will personally shower and massage you – all over."

She smiled. When Sandra smiles the room lights up and the Moon gets jealous.

"Would you help me put my shoes on?" She asked in her best imitation of a vamp.

I showered first, and changed into a pair of dress slacks and a knit sweater. It was half past six when we headed out. She was still wearing the clothes she'd worn to school, but to me she looked as sexy as a top model.

It took nearly an hour to drive to Little River Turnpike in Annandale, Virginia, and she rested her head on my shoulder all the way. Her hair smelled of some flowery shampoo. It tickled my nose. Her nearness; the warmth of her body against my arm; tickled something else, but I forced myself to keep my mind on my driving.

We went to a place just off Little River Turnpike called 'Seoul Palace.' It was crowded when we arrived, mostly Korean families or local Korean businessmen. The families were eating in traditional Korean style, with main dishes in the center of the table being shared by everyone, and more than a dozen side dishes scattered around, many of them pungent *kimchi* in different varieties. The men were eating, but there were more bottles of *soju*, the Korean equivalent of Japanese *sake*, and glasses were touching lips frequently. Other than a group of four white women sitting at a corner table, picking tentatively at the *kimchi* and making faces, we were the only non-Koreans. We'd eaten there before, though, and the waitress at the front remembered us. She gave us a table near the kitchen, took our drink and food orders, and disappeared. A young Hispanic-looking man, probably Salvadoran, delivered our drinks, large bottles of *OB* beer, a well-known Korean brew, and two glasses.

I poured for both of us. The first drink went down smoothly, as my first drink of the day always does. Sandra made a face after taking a sip.

"No matter how often I drink this stuff," she said. "It still tastes bitter."

"That's just the formaldehyde they use to age it," I said. I laughed to let her know I was just joking. That was an old joke GIs used to flog in Vietnam to explain the bitter taste of *33* or *ba moui ba*, the most-often-served beer in the dives frequented by U.S. soldiers. She didn't laugh.

"I've never tasted formaldehyde, but this

does taste like the stuff they use in the lab at school to preserve frog specimens. I can't wait for the food to arrive so it can wash the taste out of my mouth."

"Would you prefer a glass of wine?"

She made an even more sour face. "No thank you. I did that last time, remember? They like their wine too sweet. Maybe I'll just have water."

I signaled the waitress, and asked for a pot of hot tea and a glass of cold water. I moved Sandra's bottle of beer to my side of the table. What can I say, it's an acquired taste.

The tea and water arrived at the same time as the food, and just as I was finishing my beer and starting on Sandra's. We'd ordered *kalbi*, or barbecued beef ribs, *mae un tang*, which is a spicy fish soup, a noodle dish called *chop chae*, and rice. There were of course, nearly twenty side dishes, some I recognized, some not. Sandra dove right in. She's a lot more adventurous with food than drink, and had taken to the spicy Korean cuisine like a duck to water.

We ate in silence for a few minutes, just long enough to take the edge off our hunger.

Then, as we'd taken to doing, we talked. Or, the one who had just finished chewing talked, while the other listened. I'd lived alone so long after my wife Sarah was killed I'd gotten out of the habit of dinnertime conversation. Sandra, in addition to showing me that I was capable of loving again, had slowly reintroduced me to that custom.

"Well," she said after she'd taken a drink of water. "What are you working on these days? You seemed a bit distracted when you came home this evening."

I told her about the Kellogs, the murder, and being hired by young Kellog to prove that his jail buddy didn't kill his fiancée.

"That must be really popular with the local police. I mean, if they think he did it, it won't look good if you prove them wrong."

"It won't look as bad as convicting the wrong person."

"You think he's innocent, or just not guilty?"

I like the way Sandra thinks. She had a good point; there's a difference between being innocent of a crime and 'not guilty.' In the first instance, you didn't commit the crime; in the second, the law can't prove you did. I thought about it for a few seconds. Was Luther Brand innocent, or was it just that with the weak circumstantial evidence against him, a good lawyer could get a 'not guilty' verdict?

All crimes, murder included, are composed of a number of elements. There's the victim, the perpetrator, opportunity, means, and motive. Proving a person guilty in my book required all these elements to line up.

In this case, what did I have? Victim: Penelope Laine. Accused perpetrator: Luther Brand. Opportunity: he could have gotten access to the guest room, but that was weak, because someone should have seen him. Means: until someone came up with the murder weapon, this remained a question mark. Motive: he and the victim, according to both him and Joseph Kellog, were friends. It didn't make sense that he'd kill a friend for a necklace, even one as valuable as the missing piece of jewelry. There was also the matter of the other jewelry not having been taken. If robbery was his motive, why would he leave it?

It didn't line up. It didn't add up. It didn't make sense.

"I think he's innocent," I said.

"Why?" The way she asked the question, looking at me with those big blue eyes of hers all innocent-like, I knew she was trying to draw me out, make me fill in the blanks of my reasoning; a lot like she did with her students at Carter High School.

"Well, my dear; except for psychopaths who get a thrill from it or who are commanded by a voice in their heads, or serial killers who have a compulsion to kill, people kill for only a few reasons – love, hate, jealousy, money, or to cover up a crime. Even contract killers do it for the money. Money is the only logical motive that could be applied to Luther Brand, but if that was it, why would he take a piece of jewelry worth a hundred-fifty thousand, and is so distinctive it would be hard to convert to cash, and leave less distinctive pieces that would be easier to fence? He might not be educated, but he's not stupid. He has to know that a black man with a rock like that would stand out like a pimple on prom night."

"So, if he didn't do it, you have to look at everyone else who had access to the scene, and find out who had what motive. You do that, and you have your killer, right?"

Right, but when your suspect list includes one of the richest men in the state, and other members of his family, you're walking on glass shards, and someone is just waiting to drop a weight on your head. I could just see myself walking into Brian O'Malley's office and saying that one of the Kellogs was the murderer, so go and arrest him or her. When he stopped laughing, he'd show me the door;

probably without bothering to open it first.

I let the question hang in the air, though. She was right. I had to get under the skin and into the mind of everyone in and around that house. One of them was a killer and rich or not, I wasn't going to just roll over and let them get away with it.

"Damn straight, babe," I said. "Now, all I have to do is pull a rabbit out of my hat and find a motive."

We finished dinner. The *kimchi* and fish soup absorbed the two bottles of beer, or at least when I told Sandra that, she accepted it and let me drive home. Part of our trip was on the Beltway, and she hates driving it. I hate it, too, but what can you do? I'm an ultra-defensive driver on Washington's Beltway when I've had nothing to drink; when I've had a couple, I drive like everyone else on the road's out to smash into me – which seems to be the case with a lot of the drivers in the area. We made it home okay.

I jumped into the shower with her, and after we'd dried off, gave her one of my special massages. We both fell asleep with smiles on our faces.

Ten

I woke up the next morning burping garlic – one of the principal ingredients in several of the dishes we'd eaten the night before. I was wishing it was Friday, or Saturday even, but it was only Thursday. I left Sandra sleeping, and dressed for my morning run.

It took a good four miles to sweat most of the garlic out of my system. You wouldn't want to have been downwind of me when I came huffing out of the woods and went to the barn for a few minutes of pounding and kicking the heavy bag I keep there. Twenty minutes of meditation and I was ready to shower.

Sandra was just coming out of the shower when I came in, dropping my clothing on the floor as I walked. As I passed her, she wrinkled her nose.

"Pe-ew, you smell like garlic," she said.

"You probably did too, before you showered. I smelled like garlic last night, but since you did too, you didn't notice – at least, you didn't complain."

She blushed.

"I had something else on my mind," she said. "Now, get cleaned up, and come out for breakfast; I'll cook this morning."

"Aren't you going to run?"

"I have to take two classes on a field trip to the Smithsonian today. Believe me; I'll get all the running I need."

Thirty minutes later, smelling like one of her scented soaps, I joined her for breakfast. She smiled her approval, and gave me extra sausage and a four-stack of pancakes.

I was feeling good when I got to the office at half past eight.

Heather was sitting at her desk, sipping tea from the mug I'd gotten her for her birthday. Today's tea smelled like mint.

"Hey, boss, about time you got to work," she said. "Pull up a chair, do I have some stuff for you."

"On the current case?"

She's good, but if she'd found something already, she was better than I gave her credit for.

"What else?"

She was better.

"Okay, what you got?"

She pulled out a steno pad and flipped it open to a page that was covered in her neat script.

"I started running a check on that Korean couple, Tongsu Park and Monghee Lee, like you asked."

"You got results back that quick?"

"Oh, it only takes a few minutes if you know where to look. Driver's licenses, marriage licenses, mortgages, credit cards, birth certificates, even social security numbers, are easy to access. I got all that on these two, but then it got a bit hinky."

Only Heather uses words like 'hinky.' Fortunately, after so many years, I know what she means.

"How . . . hinky?" I asked.

"Well, based on credit card activity and all the other things people do, they didn't exist before December 1980. I mean, there was nothing . . . nada."

"Maybe that's when they came to the U.S. from Korea? The Korean files might not be on the Internet."

"Possibly, but I checked with a friend of mine at INS; the Immigration and Naturalization Service hasn't put many its records on line yet. They still use paper and microfiche. Anyway, even accounting for the variations of Korean names, they have no record of either of them entering the United States any time in the past thirty years, either as immigrants or visitors. Besides, they had birth certificates on file; he was born in Baltimore in 1952, and she was born in Philadelphia in 1960. But, other than the birth certificates, there's no record of them doing anything until 1980; no school records, no nothing."

That got my attention. I knew where it was going, but had to ask.

"You're saying they're not who they claim to be?"

"Well, let's just say I got curious. So, I decided to look up death certificates. There was a Tongsu Park born in Baltimore on February 13, 1952, and a Monghee Lee in Philadelphia on September 28, 1960. But, he died at the age of five of complications from pneumonia, and she drowned in the bathtub when she was three."

"Didn't they start working for Kellog around that time?"

"I can't confirm the exact date, but it was late 1980 or early 1981 based on their tax returns."

This bit of information added a completely new wrinkle to my investigation. If Park and Lee were not Park and Lee – and I had no doubt that Heather's finds were valid – then, who were they, and what were they up to?

Identity theft isn't a new crime, and using the names of infants who died around the same time you were born to obtain copies of birth certificates, social security numbers, and other identity documents is a scam that dates back to the 1970s and probably earlier. It's called paper chasing, and since birth records are maintained by states, there's no central registry to check if the perpetrator has crossed state lines. In fact, unless someone like Heather starts digging into someone's background, there was seldom any cross-checking of such cases. The biggest drawback to doing this is, if someone does check, and happens to run across the death certificate, you're busted. Apparently no one had checked these two for twenty years.

Now, though, I had to decide what to do about it.

"Heather," I said. "I want you to check

Kellog's company, and see if he does any work for the government, especially sensitive or classified contracts for the military."

She made a note on her pad. "Check. Anything else?"

"Yeah, see what Korean files you can dig up around the 1980 time frame. I don't know Korean well enough to know if these two are from the north or south. See if there was anything happening around that time that might explain how and why they ended up in the U.S., and most importantly, working for Jackson Kellog."

"You think they might be spies?

I shrugged. "Let's see what you dig up. What did you find on Wilson?"

"His file is thicker, him being in the Marines and all. He was a force recon, whatever the heck that is. Got out before twenty, though, a general discharge. I'm not sure what that means."

"It means he was dirty, but they didn't have enough to court martial his ass, so they just kicked him to the curb. Any idea what it was about?"

"There wasn't a lot of detail. He was accused of dealing drugs to the guys in his unit, but they never found any solid evidence, and none of the men would testify against him."

There went my respect for a fellow veteran. Of course, he could have cleaned up his act after getting booted. Yeah, and a bear doesn't shit in the woods.

"Anything on him after he left the Marines?"

"Yeah, he went to work for one of those private security firms, mostly working in South America doing security for foreign executives, but after three years, he quit and started his own company. Not a lot on that, other than the fact that his client list reads like the Fortune 500."

I just added one more name to my potential suspect list. I couldn't think of a motive; I just don't like military guys who betray their oath any more than I like dirty cops.

Eleven

At a quarter past ten I was sitting across from Quincy's desk in his office.

"You sure about this?" he asked after I told him what Heather had learned about Park and Lee.

"Quince, you know Heather doesn't make mistakes when it comes to ferreting out information on people," I said. "These two have taken the identities of two kids who died young. The question is, why?"

His expression turned serious.

"That means they're illegal aliens. That puts it in the hands of the feds."

"Yeah, but if they're involved in Penelope Laine's murder, bringing the feds in could really screw up the investigation. That would leave Luther Brand on the hook. I'm not prepared to do that; not just yet."

We'd already had the conversation about my belief in his innocence. Quincy gave me the lecture about my tendency to see myself as a knight in shining armor, coming to the rescue of the downtrodden. I hadn't argued with him. Hell, if I don't do it, who will? Not the government, that's for sure.

"So, what are you going to do?" he asked.

"Well, for now, I'm just gonna keep Heather digging to see what else turns up."

"You know, this puts me in a difficult position. I'm an officer of the court, and if I have knowledge of a crime and don't report it, I could be in deep shit."

Quincy's not one to use even mild profanity. He only curses when he's worried. He's a friend, and I didn't want to get him in trouble.

"Look, you don't really *know* a crime's been committed," I said. "You just heard me speculating. Who knows, maybe Heather made a mistake. After all, Korean names are confusing for a westerner, right?"

That seemed to ease his mind. His expression relaxed.

"If you should find out more, I mean, confirm that there has been a violation of federal law, if I should happen to know about it, I would be duty bound to report it."

That was as close as he would come to telling me to keep such information away from him unless I was prepared to talk to the feds. I wasn't sure what I would do. I suppose it depended upon what I learned.

"Sure, I understand," I said. "What I can't figure, though, is why they would want to work for someone like Kellog."

"Go figure," he said, shrugging. "Maybe it's like the purloined letter. What better place to hide than in plain sight? Immigration's not likely to raid his compound, you know."

Made a perverted kind of sense, but it wasn't what I wanted to know. I needed some hints as to what they might be up to. Were they criminals on the run, spies, or what? Could one or both of them be involved in Penny Laine's murder? Questions, questions, and more questions, but, no answers.

Quincy and I chatted about odds and ends, mostly some firm cases he wanted me to look at when I had time, and then I left. I'd promised to meet my other friend, Buster Mayweather for lunch.

I haven't known Buster as long as Quincy, but in some ways, he's closer. It was he who came to my house with two uniformed cops the night my wife and son were killed, who had gone with me to the morgue in Arlington

to identify their smashed and mutilated
bodies, and who had sat with me all night as
I alternated between howling at the wall and
staring at it in a semi-catatonic state. That
experience had, like combat, bonded us. He
and his wife Alma were, for a long time, the
family I no longer had. They fell in love with
Sandra when they met her, and when their
twins were born, not only made Sandra and I
the god parents, but named them after us.

Buster and I met two or three times a
month for lunch at a place on Sixteenth
Street called 'Mom's', a soul food joint that
has been a fixture in the neighborhood for as
long as anyone can remember.

I'd thrown caution to the wind and driven
the bug, now christened the Bug because of
its green color, to K Street to meet Quincy. I'd
charge the parking fee to Kellog's account
since I'd gone to see Quincy to discuss the
case. The drive from K Street to Sixteenth can
be a bit tricky during the middle of the day
because of traffic flow. I could have gone
down K and turned on Sixteenth, but if you
catch a backup, you can sit in traffic until
your beard grows, so I went west on K to
Washington Circle, and then northeast on
New Hampshire, which is longer in physical
distance, but quicker.

For a change, even though it was after
twelve, I beat Buster, who is usually well into

his meal by the time I arrive. Mom, all two-hundred-eighty pounds of her, wrapped in a dark green one-piece dress with a white apron around her waist that would easily serve as a two-man pup tent, greeted me when I walked through the door.

"Well, as I live and breathe," she said. "If it ain't my favorite man. Welcome, hon. Is that no good friend of yours comin' too?"

"Sure is," I said. "In fact, I'm surprised he's not already here."

"You just sit yourself down, and I'll get you a cup of coffee. Then, when he come I fix you two up with some lunch."

That's the way it is with Mom. Like the proprietors of some Italian restaurants, she insists on ordering for her favorite customers. I'd learned to never argue with her. Besides, she'd never given me a bad meal.

I was halfway through a cup of coffee, containing a touch of chicory in Mom's inimitable southern style, when Buster walked in. He looked glum.

"What's up, bub?" I asked as he plopped down in a chair facing me.

He made a growling sound, which caused a few heads to turn our way. Buster is six-one and weighs two-twenty, mostly muscle. He keeps his head shaved, and had lately taken to wearing a slight Fu Manchu mustache, which made him look menacing. Hell, he is menacing. He'd played college football, but had missed out on making a pro team when he blew his knee out. So, he came back to DC and joined the police force. Over the years he'd gone back and forth between homicide and the gang task force. He'd recently made lieutenant, and was being considered for a command, but was clinging to his job back with the gang unit.

"Oh, Alma's been givin' me a bunch of shit," he said.

"That sweet little thing? How can you say that?"

That sweet thing weighed about one-twenty, and was seven inches shorter than Buster, but she intimidated the hell out of him. Like a wasp nest, she was small and round, and stung like hell when agitated.

"She means well, but ever since I had my physical, she been drivin' me crazy."

"Medical problems?"

"Nothin' really serious," he said. "My cholesterol's a little high, and my tri-, triglycles -"

"Triglycerides?"

"Yeah, that. They a bit high too. So now,

Charles Ray

Alma won't buy meat 'cept chicken and fish. She make me eat vegetables and shit all the time. You know how I like me some steak, bacon, and sausage. And, I don't like eatin' the food my food eats 'less it's collards with a bit of fat back. I don't mind a bit of fried fish or chicken, but she won't fry it for me anymore."

"She's just trying to protect your health; make sure you live a long, healthy life."

Mom waddled over. She patted Buster's bald head.

"You want coffee, right?"

He nodded.

"Okay, comin' right up and yo food be right behind it."

He smiled for the first time since walking through the door.

"Now, why can't more women be like Mom? She knows how to feed a man."

"I'll admit the food here's good, but it's pumping more fat into your bloodstream than is good for you."

"Yeah, but it make you feel good."

He had a point there; Mom cooked her food the same way she had for decades, which meant it was fried – although, she did

110

now use vegetable oil instead of lard – and she put pieces of fat meat in vegetables for flavor. Fortunately for both of us, we only ate there infrequently, which hopefully gave our arteries time to flush the fat between visits.

"I wonder what her special is today."

"Don't matter," Buster said. "It'll be good. Now, you only invite me to eat when you want somethin'. What you gone get me in trouble about this time?"

"Well, it just so happens that the only thing I need from you today is advice."

He laughed; a booming sound that turned heads again.

"Now if that don't beat all. The famous Brown Knight want advice from me. What's it about; your live life?"

Buster liked poking at me over the nickname my Washington Post reporter friend Lucy Mendez had given me because of my help to people in Washington who didn't often get much help. I'd almost gotten used to it. As for my love life, taking his advice in that area struck me as about as useful as taking marriage advice from a celibate priest.

"No, it's about a case I'm working on."

I gave him a pretty detailed summary of the case, including the latest information

Heather had dug up.

"You sure, you don't think this dude Luther Brand's innocent 'cause he's black?" Then he shook his head. "Naw, forget I said that. That ain't your style. So, what you think happened?"

"Damned if I can figure it out. Problem is, a lot of people had the opportunity, but the cops can't find the weapon – hell, they don't even know what it is – and, I can't figure out a motive. This situation with the two Koreans is troubling, because other than the bullshit burglary story the cops have for justifying looking at Brand, I'm thinking that if Laine tumbled to their status, they might have offed her to keep her from talking. Then, there's the chief of security. He has a general discharge from the Marine Corps, and suspicions of having dealt in drugs before."

"Hell, man; that's as much a stretch as the burglary story. Whoever heard of an illegal alien killing to cover up sneakin' into the country? And, lot of GIs I know done drugs. If they didn't give the dude a bad conduct, they ain't had nothin' on him, you dig. Either he innocent, or he too smart. If he can fool the Marines, you think some chick gone tumble to him? I don't think so. You got to come up with somethin' better than that."

"I know, but that shows you how

desperate I am, that I'd come up with bullshit like that. I'm sort of up against a brick wall on this one. Quincy thinks I should tell the feds about the Koreans and let them handle it. What do you think?"

"I say fuck it. The feds got all the budget, and they always lookin' down their noses at us local fuzz. Let 'em do they own work. If you find out these two done broke some other law, that's different. I look 'round this town, and what I see is, if they make all the people what ain't got papers go home, lots of companies gone have to close their doors. Who gone cut all them rich folks' lawns? We got enough to do enforcing local laws."

While I pondered his advice, Mom brought our lunch. Actually, she called it dinner, because in her world, lunch was in a box that you took to work or school. It smelled deadly. Chicken fried steak, okra, mashed potatoes, and little fried corn cakes with sweet corn, chopped onions and peppers in them. I quit pondering and we began eating. It was good, probably unhealthy as hell, but damn good. Buster looked like he'd died and gone to heaven.

We had coffee with the meal, and lemonade to cleanse our palates, and just enjoyed each other's company for over an hour. Buster left before I did; his office called his cell to alert him to a suspect they'd been chasing, who was holed up in a vacant building not too far from us. I finished the last of my lemonade, kissed Mom on a pudgy cheek and drove back to the office.

Heather looked flustered when I walked in.

"Boss, pull up a chair," she said. "You need to be sitting for this."

"What's got your knickers in a knot, honeybunch?" I asked, using the name she'd only let me get away with.

"You asked me to check on events in Korea around 1980, and look into Kellog's business. I've been doing that all morning, and what I've found is interesting."

I straddled the chair at her desk.

"Okay, entertain me."

"Well, let's start with the Korean situation. The 1980s were a turbulent time there. General Park Chunghee, who'd run the country since he staged a coup in 1961, was assassinated by his intelligence chief in 1979. Another general, Chun Doowhan, took over, and not only was he as much a dictator as Park, but he was a greedy, avaricious, evil man. Shortly after he took power, there was an uprising of students and workers in the southern city of Kwangju. Chun sent the army in and hundreds were killed. He then declared martial law."

"Sounds like the country went from the frying pan into the wok," I said.

She ignored my lame attempt at humor. Okay, it wasn't all that funny, and probably didn't make any sense, but I *am* her boss; you'd think she'd consider that sometimes, but she never does.

"He did jump start Korea's industrial development, though. He shifted them to high-tech, automobiles, ships, and computers. Today, they're giving the Japanese a run for their money, and since the country went democratic, the economy has been growing at a phenomenal rate."

"Okay, so you got a country that went from a basket case to an economic powerhouse in twenty years; what does that have to do with Park and Lee?"

"I'm not sure, but it does have something to do with Jackson Kellog. Kellog started a plastics company in 1978, just two years after there was even such a thing as the plastics industry. While all of the companies were innovative, much like the computer companies, he was a real 'push the edge of the envelope' type; making components for cars, appliances, and most of all computers. The stuff the companies were putting out are the reason we have smaller, more powerful computers today, and they were a boon to the auto industry. Kellog's company has a hundred patents for plastic components that are used by industry and the government."

I was having a problem making the connection she'd obviously already made.

"All right, clue me in; what's the connection?"

"A country is trying to improve its industry. Plastics are the key to the sectors they're interested in. Kellog makes plastic components. Getting someone inside his organization could mean millions, even billions in income."

"Industrial espionage," we both said, looking at each other.

Unfortunately, it was all too credible. Back in 1976, South Korean politicians, working through the Korean Central Intelligence Agency and a Korean businessman residing in the U.S., Tongsun Park, had funneled bribes to members of Congress in an effort to influence U.S. actions regarding the possible withdrawal of American soldiers from South Korea. With the stench of Watergate still hovering over Washington, when word of this hit the airwaves; especially when it was learned that possible more than 100 members of Congress had received payments as high as $200,000, it quickly exploded into a full-scale scandal.

Americans, though, have a short attention span, and this was quickly forgotten. Asians, I knew, were not so short sighted, and it's doubtful that the new military rulers in 1980 had lost sight of Korea's objective to improve its economy, or had developed an aversion to doing whatever necessary to achieve that objective.

A theory began forming. Given the circumstances, my suspicions of Tongsu Park, and the similarity in names with the central figure in the Koreagate scandal wasn't lost on me, and Monghee Lee, didn't seem all that far-fetched anymore. If Penelope Laine had somehow learned of their deception, it didn't seem beyond the realm of possibility that she would be killed to avoid exposure.

Proving it, though, wouldn't be easy.

One thing I needed to do was find a subtle way to approach Jackson Kellog with this information. If his company was under threat, even though he wasn't my client, he had a right to know.

I gave Heather a peck on the cheek in reward for her find, and went into my office to mull over what we'd learned, and map out my next moves.

I was hardly settled behind my desk when

the intercom buzzed. I stabbed the red button.

"Yeah, Heather, what is it?"

"Quincy just called," she said. "He needs you to deliver some documents to a client in Norfolk. He apologized for the short notice, but they have to be in the client's hands by close of business tomorrow; signed and returned to Quincy by Monday morning. He's sending them over by messenger now."

"Damn, that means a whole day driving down, and either staying overnight, or driving back in the middle of the night."

"He suggests you spend the night. He had his secretary make a reservation for you at Hampton Inn. The firm's paying for it, and they'll pay mileage and per diem to make up for disrupting your schedule."

I couldn't argue with that. Extra money is extra money. I could take off from home at sunup, and even with traffic on the Interstates, make Norfolk by early afternoon. Friday night there, and be back home by mid-afternoon on Saturday. Sandra wouldn't be able to get a day off on such short notice, so I'd have to make it up to her before and after the trip. That, I thought, should be fun.

"Well," I said. "In that case, I think I'll knock off early and go home. Call me if there's an emergency."

She laughed. In more than a decade, other than the time when two thugs broke in to see if we had any evidence of their art theft ring, we'd had no emergencies.

Just before leaving, I decided to call Joseph Kellog.

"I need to speak with your father," I said when he answered.

"Can you tell me what it's about?" he asked.

"I think I'd better talk to him. If he wants to share it with you, that's his call."

He asked me to hang on, and I heard a rustling sound as he carried his cell phone from his office to his father's, two doors down the hall. He must have had his hand over the speaker, because I could hear voices, but they were muffled.

"What can I do for you, Mr. Pennyback," Jackson Kellog's voice boomed in my ear.

I told him what we'd learned about Park and Lee, and asked him if his company had ever had any problems with theft of their trade secrets, or any other issues.

There was a long period of silence. At first, I thought perhaps he'd put the phone down.

"Mr. Pennyback," his voice had a weary tone when he finally spoke. "You're barking up the wrong tree. Thomas and Mary have worked for me for twenty years. They are absolutely loyal. The very idea that they'd do anything to hurt me or my business is repellent."

"That might be so," I said. "But, there's still the issue of the gaps in their lives. How do you explain that?"

"I . . . can't . . . and, I have no intention or desire to do so. Take my advice, Mr. Pennyback; look elsewhere. There's nothing to be gained from prying into their lives. Trust me, to do so would be a mistake."

Then, he did break the connection. I wasn't sure if I'd just received a warning, or a plea, but it piqued my curiosity. And, that's the wrong thing to do. I'm a sucker for puzzles, and he'd just handed me one hell of a puzzle to solve. And, by God, I wasn't going to stop until I solved it.

Twelve

I got home an hour before Sandra, and by the time she arrived, I had supper prepared. I'd made a pot of my five-alarm chili, with corn bread and a tossed salad, which we washed down with ice-cold *dos equis* beer.

After the kitchen was cleaned, we retired to the living room with two more beers and listened to the early evening NPR broadcast, a program of Beethoven's sonatas, and I told her my plans for Friday and Saturday.

"Damn," she said. "Why couldn't Quincy ask you to do that on Saturday so I could go with you?"

"Don't worry, babe, I'll make it up to you Saturday night when I get back."

"You'll start making it up to me tonight, buster." The look in her eyes told me I wouldn't be getting much sleep.

But, it was worth it.

So was the way she woke me up the next morning. I did a quick run and meditation, and after showering, just ate toast, jam and coffee. I was on the road by 7:30.

The Beltway was a mess, but by the time I got to I-95 south, the traffic had thinned. Except for watching out for the 18-wheelers that were running in packs and playing chicken with smaller vehicles, it was a pleasant drive to Richmond, where I took I-64 south to the coast. It was nearing 1:30 when I got to the I-664 beltway that encircled Norfolk, and I had to fight traffic until I was near the big naval base.

I found the client in an office park a few blocks from the main gate of the base. He took the sealed manila envelope Quincy's messenger had delivered, and told me he'd get a signed document to me at my hotel that evening. I knew that could mean any time before midnight, so I checked into the Hampton and kicked back in my room watching old movies on the cable channel.

At 6:30, I called Sandra. We chatted about nothing in particular for ten minutes; she told me she missed me, and I said I missed her even more. We both rang off before it got too mushy, and I walked across the street from the motel and had a fried chicken special at a Popeye's.

An envelope was waiting for me when I got back to the motel. It was too late to drive back to Washington, and since Quincy's firm had already paid for the hotel, I decided to get an early start, so I went to bed early.

Saturday morning, I got up at sunrise, had coffee and a bagel in the motel lobby, checked out, and got on the road. Even though it was Saturday, and the sun was just coming up, traffic in the Norfolk area was heavy. It lightened up near Richmond, and during the drive north on I-95, I only had to contend with the trucks. Doesn't seem to matter which direction, or which time of day, I-95 is like a demolition derby with the long-haul trucks driving ten to fifteen miles over the speed limit, belching diesel fumes, throwing off pieces of tire, and scaring the crap out of other motorists.

The Bug got good gas mileage. I only had to fill up once, and made good time, getting home before four. Sandra was curled up on the sofa grading papers when I walked in. She looked as happy to see me as I was to see her.

The papers were left scattered on the floor in front of the sofa, while I made up to her as I'd promised.

Thirteen

After a relaxing weekend when Sandra and I did little beyond get up on Sunday and do a quick run, followed by thirty minutes on the heavy bag where I gave her a few more karate lessons, shower together, which left the bathroom floor covered in water, and then a leisurely breakfast, which we prepared together. We spent the rest of the day just lolling around and enjoying the quiet and each other's company.

So, when Monday came, after a run and breakfast, I was ready to kick ass.

"How was Norfolk?" Heather asked when I breezed through the door.

I just shrugged. Except for the traffic, the business park, and my motel, I'd not seen much of it; hadn't wanted to really.

"You get anything new on Friday?" I asked.

"Nothing more on the two Koreans. They're like phantoms; without a name or something, I don't even know where to start looking, so I decided to look deeper into the Kellog background."

"I hope you found something useful. I'm starting to get frustrated with this case. There's a ton of suspects, but no real motives to help narrow the field."

She gave me her innocent look, meaning what she'd found was probably not useful to the investigation, but was nevertheless fascinating. Like most computer geeks, who are artists at heart, the beauty of information often has little to do with its utility.

"Well, let's start with the old man, shall we," she said in her best professorial tone. "You needn't be reminded that he's worth billions, that's with a 'b', not an 'm', as in about ten billion dollars when the stock market closed on Friday.

She opened her steno pad. The page she flipped to was covered in neat columns of figures interspersed with her neat handwriting.

"He's been at the front of most of the

innovations in the plastics industry from the beginning," she continued. "He was one of the first, for instance, to recognize that the conductivity of plastic was a key to controlling overheating of computer components. There's hardly a computer of any size today that doesn't have at least one component made by Kellog's company. Same thing with automobiles and appliances; he saw early that plastic parts would be a way to cut down on weight and increase efficiency."

"So, the guy's the Thomas Edison of plastics? I already knew he was rich," I said petulantly. "How does this help me figure out who killed Penny Laine?"

"You know, boss; for a man who meditates, you're awfully impatient. If you'll let me tell the story my way, it will become clear. Now, where was I? Oh yeah, he became a leader in the industry. His company sells plastic parts to the world. And, that world includes South Korea. Remember I told you that in 1980, the new military government changed the country's industrial priorities, with an emphasis on high-technology and computers?"

A light, albeit a dim bulb, came on in my mind.

"The Koreans were customers for Kellog's products?"

"Big time; but only for a year. He sold millions of dollars' worth of plastic products between mid-1979 until around the end of 1980, and then suddenly, it was like the pipeline dried up. Shipments to Korea dropped almost eighty percent."

"Don't tell me," I said. "It had nothing to do with a drop in Korean demand."

"Not at all. In fact, the demand went up. The Koreans had to look for other suppliers."

"Why did Kellog stop selling to them?"

"I'm still trying to track that down," she said. "The old man's history with Korea, though, goes back to way before that. During the Korean War, he enlisted in the army. He was with the Third Infantry Division. Fought at a place called the Chosin Reservoir. That was a battle where most of the Americans, the army in the east and the Marines in the west, were wiped out by the Chinese. Kellog got the Silver Star for that battle."

I didn't need the history lesson; everyone who serves in the military is given frequent training that includes the history and lineage of the service. The battle at Chosin Reservoir during the Korean War, when an outnumbered American force of army and marines, surrounded by the Communist Chinese, not only broke out of the encirclement, but inflicted heavy casualties on the enemy in the process, is used to demonstrate the importance of never giving up or giving in. Like Iwo Jima and Bastogne in World War II, it's considered a key point in American military history.

"I'm not surprised. He impressed me as a tough old buzzard."

"There was one interesting incident. I haven't been able to get all the details; but apparently Kellog and his Korean interpreter were trapped for three days behind enemy lines. They managed to evade the Chinese and make it back to their headquarters. The information they brought back helped the Americans in their withdrawal from the area. Anyway, after the war, Kellog made a trip to Korea every year in April. He stayed for a month each time. He did this until 1980. That year, he made two trips; one in April, and one in September. He hasn't been back since."

"Well, that's understandable," I said. "He's tough, but he *is* in his seventies after all. That's a long flight, and it can't be easy for him."

She laughed and waggled her finger at me.

"Not so, boss; not so. He goes big game hunting in South Africa every December. That's got to be tougher than flying to Korea."

"Yeah, you're right. I wonder why he broke his pattern and made that second trip."

"Why he made it is a mystery," she said. "How he made it is stranger still."

"How so?"

"He flew out of San Francisco to Seoul's Kimpo Airport, as usual. This time, though, he only stayed for a week, then he cashed in his return air ticket and took a Liberian freighter crewed by Filipinos out of the southern port city of Pusan. A month later, he crossed the Mexican border at Brownsville, Texas."

"Let me guess; there's no information about what he did during that month."

She snapped her fingers. "Dang, boss, you're almost as smart as me. Fact is, there's nothing about his activities from the time he cleared immigration at Kimpo. What he did, where he went, or who he met in Korea is unknown, and there's zilch about his activity between Korea and Texas."

This was becoming as irritating as a cocklebur in your boots, or a scratch in the finish of a new car. The more I learned about Jackson Kellog, the more questions were raised. He was becoming a puzzle wrapped in a riddle and tied up with an enigma, or something like that. If I was the emotional type, it would have been pissing me off. It was time to have another face-to-face talk with him, and I didn't think the conversation would be pleasant.

But, Heather wasn't done.

"One other thing, which probably has nothing to do with anything," she said. "But, Jennifer Kellog was admitted last year to a rehab facility in Philadelphia. I couldn't find any details on why, but she spent six weeks there."

One could fill a book; a whole shelf of books; with this family's trials and tribulations. My head was beginning to spin at the sheer volume of stuff Heather was unearthing; but no threads connecting any of it to the murder were showing themselves.

I called Jackson Kellog and informed him that I would be arriving in his office sometime after lunch; that I had some questions for him, and I wouldn't be letting up until I got answers that made sense.

He didn't sound at all happy, but he didn't tell me not to come, nor did he indicate that I wouldn't be admitted to his tightly-guarded compound.

Fourteen

I was admitted to the compound. The guard even smiled and saluted. I guess I was on the cleared list. Of course, he still did the full search of my car, including the sniffer dog. I'd left the flares at home this trip.

The Korean housekeeper, still frowning at me as if I was a wet dog that had been playing in a mud puddle, let me in and jerked her head toward the hall down which I would find Kellog's office. She spun on her heels and walked away before I could thank her.

Kellog was waiting for me, still sitting behind his desk with a frown on his face, still waving me toward the chair sitting in front of his desk. Still playing his dominance games. Some habits are hard to break. He toyed with a Lucite letter opener that rested in a wooden cradle on his desk as I approached.

I sat on the chair normally, rather than straddling it, but I leaned back in a relaxed posture, and looked at him, my face impassive. The one thing I've found most people can't deal with is silence. If you sit looking at them long enough, they'll cave and say something. It's like playing chicken; the first one to blink loses.

Kellog lost.

"Well, Mr. Pennyback, what is it that's so urgent that you need to talk to me about." The petulant tone in his voice told me that he'd recognized my ploy, and wasn't happy at being sucked in by it.

I let the silence linger a while longer, just until his petulant look began to shift toward anger.

"Just a few pieces of information that don't add up," I said. "Time lines that have unexplained gaps, strange travel patterns."

"Are you still on about Thomas and Mary? I told you; you're wasting time on that. Neither of them had anything to do with that poor girl's death."

"In my line of work, I find it useful never to discount any possibility. And, you have to admit, covering up illegal immigrant status, and who knows what else, could be considered a motive to try and shut someone up."

His face turned red. He seemed to be exerting a great effort to control his emotions.

"Look; they've been working for me for twenty years. I think I know them much better than you, and I assure you, they wouldn't murder anyone, not even for the reasons you state."

That was as close as he'd come; probably as close as he'd ever come; to admitting that he knew their illegal status. I decided to change tack.

"Then, there's your own activity, Mr. Kellog," I said. "For instance, from the end of the Korean War until 1980, you visited Korea annually. Then, without any explanation, your visits stopped. Why is that?"

His eyes widened, and then, narrowed. He regarded me intently for a few seconds.

"You're a very resourceful man. How did you discover that information?"

"Like you said, I'm resourceful." I saw no reason to tell him about Heather. "I know a lot about you, but what I've learned only causes me to have more questions. For instance, your last visit; you left Korea by ship, but didn't come back to the U.S. for a month."

"That's not so unusual," he said. "I hopped a ride on a freighter that's part of a company we do business with. It wasn't exactly an ocean liner. The voyage took 21 days."

"But, you came back by way of Mexico."

"That particular vessel didn't have any U.S. ports of call. I got off at the first port, which just happened to be in Mexico. The ship went on to Chile from there, and I came home."

He was giving me information, while at the same time, withholding. If the freighter was bound for Chile, that meant it stopped at one of the Mexican ports on the Pacific. It would have been more logical for Kellog to re-enter the U.S. through a California border point; yet, he crossed the width of the country and came back through Texas, and not even a main crossing like El Paso. The upshot of it was, he was talking, but not really answering my questions.

I was beginning to form a picture in my mind, but I didn't want to expose my hole cards too early. I also didn't want to accuse the old man without more to go on. He was, after all, a decorated combat veteran, and that counted for something in my book.

"You fought in Korea?"

The changed in subject caught him by surprise, but only for a heartbeat.

"Yeah," he said. "I was with 3d Battalion, 15th Infantry Regiment of the Third Division." He took on a wistful, slightly sad look; one I've seen many times in war veterans – one that others have probably seen on occasion on my face.

"Must have been tough. You were at Chosin Reservoir?"

"Yeah." He nodded, remembering. "November and December 1950. We'd crossed into North Korea around November 27 with 30,000 UN troops under major General Almond. The damned Chinese crossed the Yalu around that time, and we found ourselves surrounded by nearly 70,000 of 'em at Chosin Reservoir.

His eyes misted over. He absent-mindedly wiped at them, fully caught up in the memories.

"You can't imagine what it was like. First of all, it was colder than I'd ever experienced in my life, sometimes dropping to near forty below. They don't call that damn place the Frozen Chosin for nothing. And, then there were the Chinese with their human wave attacks. We'd kill them by the hundreds, and they'd just keep on coming. Nothing worked right. Medicine froze up, vehicles froze, and men froze. The roads weren't much more than icy tracks cut through terrain so rough a mule would have trouble with it.

He stopped talking for a moment, his hands shaking. After taking a deep breath, he regarded me levelly.

"They call that battle one of the most decisive of the war. Hell, it was just 17 days of misery and death, and not all from enemy fire. Men got frostbite, or died when jeeps or trucks went off icy roads. I got separated from my unit one night during the fourth day of battle. Hadn't been for my Korean interpreter, a KATUSA named No Taedong, I would have either been killed or captured by the Chinese, or frozen to death. He kept me alive and we finally made it back to our lines. I got a medal for the information we brought back. By rights, that medal should have gone to him. Anyway, we broke out of the Chinese encirclement. Killed thousands of Chinese. Lost thousands of Americans too."

I was beginning to get a sense of the reason for his trips to Korea. From the time of the Korean War, Korean military personnel called KATUSA, or Korean Augmentation to the U.S. Army, had served alongside Americans in South Korea. Under combat conditions, differences in culture and race get ignored. Kellog's experience at Chosin would have established a bond between him and No that was stronger than even blood ties.

"Was No the reason for your visits to Korea?" I asked.

He nodded. "Yes. He was older than me by five or ten years; I never really knew his real age. After the war, he left the army and opened a noodle shop in Seoul. Barely made enough to keep his family together, but he managed to raise a son who later joined the Korean army. I helped out when I could, but he was a proud man. Hated accepting charity, even when I told him it was small repayment for his saving my life. Taedong was the closest thing to an older brother I've ever had."

"I assume he died, and that's the reason you stopped going to Korea?"

He nodded. "Yeah, he died." He blinked back unshed tears.

I waited, but that was all he would say. He sat there, staring off at something in the distance, far beyond the room.

I didn't know what he'd been up to, but at that moment, I no longer cared. He'd suffered in ways that the average person can't imagine, and I wasn't about to add to it. Call it ingrained respect for a fellow veteran; you'd be right. If I have a blind spot, it's a tendency to give comrades in arms the benefit of the doubt.

I thanked him for seeing me at such short notice, shook his dry, brittle hand, and left. He was still sitting behind his desk toying with the letter opener when I softly pulled the door shut.

Fifteen

Tuesday morning, Heather was busy at her computer and I was sitting at my desk, alternating between letting the computer trounce me at Internet chess and gazing out the window at the trees decked out in gold, orange and red.

We were at that point in a case when you have tons of information, none of it making any sense, and you feel like you've come up to the face of a sheer cliff with no handholds for getting to the top of the mountain.

Some people, when they face a situation like that, get frustrated. Frustration can cause rash behavior, leading to mistakes that put you further in a hole. When Heather reaches that point, she just dives back into the ether, working to coax even more information from the billions of electronic files that someone's keeping on all of us. Me; I just sit somewhere and think. Not the brain-aching, concentration kind of thinking. No, I just sort of turn my mind on idle and let it run. You could call it a form of active meditation. Whatever you call it, it works for me – most times.

In the current case, it was slow kicking in; hell, it wasn't kicking in at all. The blank spaces remained blank. Nothing popped out of the mass of data and said, 'here, look at me, I'm the clue you need to solve this thing.'

I'd turned away from the computer and was gazing at a little cloud of leaves that had given up and severed their connection with their home branch, and were now swirling through the October air, when I heard my door open. I swiveled my chair around. Heather was standing there.

"There's someone here to see you, boss," she said quietly.

Her tone was, 'this is important, so please say yes.'

"Send him or her in," I said.

She looked relieved as she backed out of the door, to be quickly be replaced by the stocky Korean man I'd seen working on the grounds of the Kellog compound, Tongsun Park.

He stopped just inside the door, his hands clasped at his waist.

"Have a seat," I said, waving him to the chair in front of my desk.

When he'd seated himself, he regarded me through narrowed eyes, but remained silent.

"What can I do for you?" I asked.

"Mr. Kellog tell me you visit him yesterday and ask about me," he said. He pronounced Kellog, Kellogu. "He say you know about how my wife and I come to United States."

He came straight to the point. Unusual for an Asian; in Asian culture, there's usually a period of warming up and idle chatter before getting to the real reason for a meeting.

"Let's just say the gaps in your histories raised some questions in my mind."

"I suppose it is no surprise that someone would notice sooner or later. It has been twenty years after all. Mr. Kellog think you believe my wife and I might have had something to do with Miss Laine's murder. I came to tell you that we did not."

He looked me straight in the eye; also uncharacteristic of an Asian. He'd either become totally westernized in his twenty years in the country, or alternatively he considered himself superior to me. I charitably opted for the former view.

"You have to admit, Mr. Park," I said. "It

144

doesn't look good for you. If your true status should become known, you could be deported."

"Being deported is not the worst thing that could happen to me, Mr. Pennyback," he said. "First thing you need to know; my real name is No Chongwu."

"You're the son of Kellog's interpreter from the Korean War."

"Yes, my father served with Mr. Kellog during war."

He then began to tell me his life story, beginning with Jackson Kellog and his father serving together at Chosin Reservoir.

"I was born during the second year of the war," he said. Given that during the early days, a lot of the fighting was in and around Seoul, his father probably wasn't that far from home. "Times were hard for Koreans then. Many starved. My father told me when I was young, though, that Mr. Kellog was so grateful for what he'd done for him during the battle, that he made sure our family always had food. Even after the war, he would come to visit each spring, and he always brought money and presents. I remember him well; he was like a strange, white-skinned uncle to me."

"So, Kellog's annual trips to Korea were to

visit your family?"

"Yes, and he also sent things. Thanks to him, I was able to finish high school and attend Seoul National University. Both he and my father were disappointed when I joined the army after graduation. They wanted me to come to America and work in Mr. Kellog's company. But, I had been so impressed with my father's stories about the war, even as a child I'd wanted to be a soldier and fight for my country."

His story was interrupted by Heather coming in with two mugs; black tea for him, coffee for me. She gave me a quizzical look. I returned it with a barely perceptible shrug.

Park; No, took a sip from his tea. He looked like a man with a heavy weight on his shoulders.

"So, you were in the Korean army," I said. "What did you do?"

"I began my career in the infantry; this would have been in 1974. Because I was a college graduate, they made me an officer. It was difficult for me, because I did not attend the military academy. Those who are from the academy are very close knit, and they resent outsiders. After a few years, I moved from the infantry to the Special Forces."

"This must have made your father proud.

I don't know that much about Korea's Special Forces, but I imagine it's as difficult to qualify for it as it is in the U.S."

"I think maybe is more difficult," he said matter-of-factly. "Korea is tough place. Is very hard to succeed in Korean army. You must remember, we are still at war with North Korea. At that time, they often sent armed invaders south across the DMZ. The Special Forces have a big job to stop them. I have had to fight North Koreans many times."

"Yes, I seem to remember reading about some of their attacks," I said. "They once even made it to Seoul, only a few miles from the presidential mansion."

"The North Koreans kill many South Koreans. For army it was always dangerous. But, I believed it was our duty to protect the people. After President Park was killed and General Chun took power, at first I thought things would be better. I was wrong. Chun Doowhan was as bad as my father said Syngman Rhee had been before General Park take over. Anyone who disagreed with government was put in jail, or worse. When students and workers in Kwangju protested against government, army was ordered to go there to restore order.

He got a faraway look on his face. His high cheekbones were bright red, and his broad forehead wrinkled.

"Army was ordered to shoot people. Many were killed. I was captain then, and commander of company. I refuse to order my unit to shoot students. My executive officer tried to relieve me of command. I shot him. Then, I had to run away, because I was called traitor. I make my way back to Seoul and get my wife; her real name is Baek Namja; and we flee to southern province of Cholla. My father had old friend in one village who hid us for many weeks. The government arrested my father and tried to make him tell where I was hiding, but he refused. I think my father able to get message to Mr. Kellog. He come back to Korea, but by then my father is dead. Mr. Kellog come to Cholla. He help me and Namja to leave Korea. We go by ship from Pusan to Mexico. Then, he hire people who bring us to United States through Arizona."

He continued to look at me as he talked, as if he wanted to see how I would react to it. I kept my expression impassive. On the one hand, he was my prime suspect, and what he was telling me only confirmed that, if Penelope Laine somehow learned of his status, he had every motive to silence her. On the other hand . . . well, for some reason, I wanted to believe him when he said he didn't do it. The problem is, I don't understand Korean culture well enough to be able to assess one's honesty. All I had to go on was gut feeling, and right at that moment, my gut was wrenched in two directions.

"Let me see if I've got this straight," I said. "You disobeyed a direct order from your military command, and then killed your executive officer and fled into hiding. Jackson Kellog helped you to sneak out of Korea and enter the United States without going through the legal formalities; making you an illegal alien. I would also imagine that, like the U.S., Korea has no statute of limitations on murder, so you'd still be a wanted man there. Did I get everything?"

His almond-shaped eyes widened.

"Yes," he said softly. "You have the facts correctly."

"Then, you're telling me that, if Joseph Kellog's fiancée happened to learn of your true status, you have a solid motive for killing her."

He sat back in the chair, frowning at me.

"Yes, I know," he said. "But, only Mr. Kellog know how my wife and I come to America. How could Miss Laine know? Mr. Pennyback, you must know whole story of my life. When I run away, my father was arrested by the army. They tried to make him tell where I was, but he refused. He refused many days, even though they beat him. He die in jail. They say it was heart attack, but I know the army killed him. Even now, Korea has democracy, but I can never go back to country that kill my father. Even so, I would not kill innocent person. I did not kill Miss Laine. I swear this on my honor."

I had to stifle a laugh. Here he'd just confessed to treason against his country, to killing a fellow officer, and of illegally living in the U.S., and he talked of honor. On the other hand, I suppose in his own way, he did think he was acting honorably. I had to give him credit for refusing to gun down civilians. And, unless he was trying misdirection, I had to give him points for coming clean. In a way, he too was a fellow veteran. I was, in a word, confused. He had to stay on my list as a viable suspect, but he'd also earned a small amount of my respect. Whoever said being a private eye was easy never had to deal with a case like this.

I figured it would help if I could verify some of what he'd told me, but Heather was running into a brick wall trying to pin down events in Korea. A lot of what we needed to know happened before the Internet, and had probably never been put into computer files, and a lot of it was probably buried deep in some secret government vaults somewhere.

I remembered, though, a chance encounter I'd had one day while filling my car one day at the little service station at Fort McNair. A brigadier general, who I didn't at first recognize, came toward me with his hand outstretched and a big smile on his face. When I grasped his hand, it clicked. The last time I'd seen Wesley Covington, he'd been a captain working in the operations section of the Army Special Warfare Command at Fort Bragg, where my special strike force team and I were based. He and I had talked from time to time, especially about his desire to get an assignment to an operational team instead of being chained to a desk as a staff officer. During these conversations, I learned that he'd been assigned to the Republic of Korea/United States Combined Forces Command in Seoul as an operations officer from 1979 to 1981. He'd often regaled me with tales of the chaos and confusion after Park Chunghee's assassination and the subsequent jockeying for control among the ROK generals.

Covington was, he'd informed me, up for his second star, and was assigned to the Pentagon as a staff director in the Operations Directorate, or J3, of the Joint Staff. We talked over old times as I filled my tank, and he'd given me his name card before I drove off and asked that I get in touch with him for coffee one day.

I'd let it slip my mind, but figured, what the hell; I can satisfy a social convention, and maybe get some useful information in the process.

I dug around in the clutter of my desk drawer until I found his card. I dialed the number. A bright sounding young air force staff sergeant answered and quickly transferred me to Covington, who was happy to have an excuse to get away from his desk. He invited me to join him for coffee in one of the coffee shops in the Pentagon's underground shopping complex.

.

Sixteen

From my office to the Pentagon, just across the Potomac River adjacent to Arlington National Cemetery, didn't take long. A brisk walk in the chill October air up Fourth Street to the Waterfront Metro station, a short ride on the Green Line to L'Enfant Plaza, where I got off and walked across the platform to catch the Yellow Line whose first stop in Virginia was the Pentagon station; the entire trip was under fifteen minutes.

At the Pentagon, I took the escalator up to the secure entrance area on the southeast side of the five-sided building.   It was the first time I'd been in the building since my retirement, but, except for the metro station, little seemed to have changed. Built between 1941 and 1943 to house the War Department, it is among the largest office buildings in the world, and serves as headquarters for the Defense Department, the Joint Chiefs of Staff, and the military secretaries and chiefs. Its over six million square feet of floor space, covering five acres, with five above-ground floors, two basements, and over 17 miles of corridors, has offices for more than 30,000 military and civilian employees. Like a self-contained city, it has its own power plant and water purification system, as well as its own police force. Even though it's in Virginia, it has five postal Zip Codes, all Washington, DC. When it was built, segregation was the law in Virginia, and Colonel Leslie Groves, who was in charge of construction, had separate dining and toilet facilities for whites and blacks installed. President Roosevelt, however, overruled Groves and ordered the 'Whites Only' signs removed. The result is that the Pentagon has twice the number of toilets of any comparably sized public building in the world, and from 1943 to 1965 was the only office building in Virginia that wasn't segregated.

The entrance area was crowded with people, many in uniform, going to and fro, some on their way to or from their offices, some heading to one of the shopping facilities in the complex, and others visiting. A tour was forming up near the check-in window, a group of goggling tourists being guided by a young Marine Corps corporal in dress uniform, who would walk backward through the building as he regaled his charges with its history and layout. A large group of what had to be defense contractors, well-groomed middle-aged white men in expensive suits, carrying bulging briefcases, waited in a corner, chatting quietly to each other.

Covington was waiting for me at the top of the escalator. He was casually dressed; casual, that is, for a senior officer in the Pentagon, wearing green dress trousers with the double black stripes of a flag officer up the leg, and a beige long sleeve shirt with black tie. A black ID tag over his left breast pocket identified his name and rank, as did the picture ID he wore on a chain around his neck. His hair was still cut close on the sides and medium length on top, much as he'd worn it when I knew him at Fort Bragg, but the medium brown was now flecked with gray.

"Al," he said, grasping my hand. "Good of you to finally drop by."

"Thanks for seeing me at such short notice, Wes. I apologize if I'm pulling you away from anything important."

"Are you kidding? Any excuse to get away from my desk is welcome. I never knew it until I got here, but a brigadier general in this place is the equivalent of a captain in a division headquarters. The only reason I don't have to fetch coffee for my boss is that he has a lieutenant colonel to do it. Let's go over to the coffee shop."

He led the way to a cafeteria to the left of the tour window. We got in a long line and finally came away with two Styrofoam cups of steaming coffee, which we took to a small table in a relatively unoccupied corner.

I looked around as I sipped the hot brew.

"Nothing much has changed in this place since I left it a decade ago," I said. "Still a lot of hurry up and wait."

He laughed.

"The military services, especially the army, underwent major reorganization after Vietnam, but some things will never change." He sipped his coffee, looking at me over the rim of the cup. "Look, let's cut to the chase. If I remember you correctly, you were never one for idle chit chat. You want something from me; the question is what?"

He'd been sharp as a young captain. He'd only gotten sharper with age and rank. I saw no sense in trying to play him.

"Yeah, I do need something from you," I said, getting straight to the point. "I'm working a case with a Korean connection, and I recall you telling me once you'd served in Korea in the eighties."

"That's right." He nodded. "I was a plans

officer in the unconventional warfare section of C3 with Combined Forces Command from 1979 to 1981. Worked out at CP Tango, that's a command post in a bunker under a mountain south of Seoul. What is it you want to know about that time?"

"I'm not really sure. I know it was a turbulent time. I'm trying to verify a story I heard about a ROK officer who was involved in the Kwangju uprising."

He laughed, a rueful chuckle, and shook his head.

"Hell, it was a turbulent time. I got there just before Park was assassinated by his intelligence chief, and believe me; the first few months after the assassination were not to be believed. They had a coup, then a counter-coup, with generals of different military academy classes lining up against each other, units engaging in fire fights, and there we were, the U.S. forces who were supposed to be helping them defend their country against a North Korean invasion, either caught in the middle, or left on the sidelines. Do you know, two divisions that were supposed to be under command of the senior CFC commander, who just happened to be an American four star, pulled out of their positions guarding avenues of approach from the DMZ, and headed for Seoul without telling us? If the North Koreans had chosen that time to invade, we'd have been caught with our pants down." He took another swig of coffee. "The Kwangju mess was just another dustup. It didn't involve or threaten U.S. forces, so we didn't really pay much attention to it."

"Do you know what happened?"

"I do after the fact," he said. "The ROKs kept a pretty tight lid on it at first. After it was over, though, and news reports started coming out, we found out what went down. Seems students and workers in the south felt the military government under Chun Doowhan was giving them the shitty end of the stick, so they sort of protested. You have to understand something about Koreans, Al; they only have two attitudes; friendly and kick down you door and set fire to hour house. Chun sent military units from the Seoul area to Kwangju to pacify people. What that means is, break some heads; and, that's exactly what they did. I'm not sure we even know how many people were killed, rioters or military. What does a Korean officer from that era have to do with a PI's case today here in the DC area?"

"Sorry, client confidentiality, Wes. But, what I heard was that an officer refused to obey orders to fire on the rioters, and deserted. You ever hear anything like that?"

His face screwed up in concentration, and he put a finger to his temple.

"Hey, now that you mention it," he said. "I did hear some stories. Didn't pay too much attention to them at the time, though. Some of the ROK SF types I worked with in C3 mentioned an incident 'down south,' which was their euphemism for Kwangju. Something about an SF commander who wouldn't fire on civilians and his deputy tried to relieve him of command. He reportedly killed the deputy and fled. Guys who talked to me were mixed in their reactions to it. To some he was a hero, an honorable military professional who took his oath to protect the people seriously. To others he was a traitor who should be taken out and shot."

"I imagine things wouldn't go too well for him if he should be discovered, even today?"

"Hard to say. Been a lot of changes in the government since the eighties. I'm not sure they'd want to be reminded of that time. Of course, a lot of the young officers who were involved in Kwangju are now senior officers, and I doubt they'd want their activities resurrected. Then, of course, there's what allegedly happened to the guy's father."

My attention perked up.

"What happened to his father?" I asked.

"Well, this is all rumor, you have to remember; but what I heard was the army beat the old man to death trying to get him to tell where his son had gone."

He was looking at me curiously now. I decided that there wasn't anything else useful he could tell me, and I wasn't ready for what I knew, or suspected I knew to become public.

"Hey, Wes," I said. "This has been really helpful. It helps me understand some things a lot better."

He didn't get to be a brigadier general just on his good looks. He was smart enough to know that I wasn't going to tell him what was going on. Unlike civilians, though, who might get their backs up at being kept in the dark, he was accustomed to the 'need-to-know' principle; if you have no specific need to know information, you don't get it.

"Glad I could be of help. Look, don't be a stranger, Al. You know, when I was a young captain, you were my role model. It's thanks to you I hung in long enough to make my first star. We should get together now and then, you know, just shoot the shit."

"I will, Wes. I'm a bit tied up right now with this case, but I promise, as soon as it's over, I'll have you out to my house for drinks. I'm assuming you're married now?"

"Yeah, and with two sons. One's in high school and one's in his second year at West Point. I seem to remember when we were at Bragg, you were married too. A Filipina girl?"

"I was; had a son too, but they were killed in an auto accident just before I retired from the army."

Sadness clouded his features. "Sorry to hear that."

That put a damper on our conversation. I didn't want to talk any more, and he seemed discomfited by my news. We finished our coffee in silence, renewed our promises to get together soon, and I headed back down to the subway station for the trip back to the office.

Seventeen

Wes Covington's story tended to corroborate Thomas Park's story – I still had trouble thinking of him as No Chongwu – but, it left me with a bit of a dilemma. It further strengthened his motive for killing Penny Laine.

One part of my mind, sympathetic to what he'd endured, wanted to believe that he was innocent, that he was in fact an honorable man who wouldn't kill an innocent woman, just as he'd refused to gun down students nearly three decades earlier. But, another part, looking at the evidence, as circumstantial as it was, was convinced almost beyond a reasonable doubt that somehow Penelope Laine had discovered his secret, and he'd killed her to keep it hidden.

Every crime needs a victim, a perpetrator, and facts that tie the perp to the crime, such as motive, means, and opportunity. In this case, I had motive aplenty. I now had to determine if there had been opportunity, and by what means he – or she - had done it.

Somehow, I had to find the weapon that killed Laine. I had a feeling it would lead directly to the killer.

While significant portions of my brain were occupied with Park's probably guilt, a smaller part kept going back to Luther Brand. Like Joseph Kellog, I believed in his innocence. Not because he was a good person; he'd done a lot of bad things in his life. But, he'd done time and paid for his past misdeeds. No, I was convinced he was innocent because, despite having opportunity, based on the testimony of Park's wife, Mary Lee, the robbery motive was weak, and when I spoke to him, there'd been no indications of evasion or lying.

This line of thought occupied my mind during the metro ride back to Waterfront, and the walk down Fourth Street to my office.

Heather was busy at her computer, so I just grunted and went into my office. Sitting behind my desk, staring at a blank computer screen, I tried to reconstruct the crime in my mind.

According to the police reports, Penelope Laine had been found on the sofa in the sitting room of the mansion's guest suite.

Other than her bloody body, the place was undisturbed. I recalled the crime scene photos that had been taken before the body was removed. It appeared that she'd probably been sitting when she was stabbed. Her watch, a Piaget with gold band; probably worth at least fifteen grand, was on her left wrist, and she still wore the engagement ring Joseph Kellog had given her; a piece of jewelry he said he'd paid sixty thousand for. She was also wearing a pair of diamond earrings whose value I couldn't even guess at, but given the watch, they were probably worth a lot. Why, if the motive was robbery, would a thief only take the diamond necklace? After she was dead, the other items would have been easy to remove.

I had a thought. I dialed the number of the medical examiner.

"Leonard Scott, here," he said. "What can I do for you?"

"Dr. Scott, Al Pennyback. Got a question for you; were there any signs on Penelope Laine's body indicating the necklace she was wearing was forcibly removed?"

"No," he replied after a few moments. "Other than the stab wound, there wasn't a mark on her body."

I thanked him and rang off.

If the necklace had been jerked off her neck in haste, there would have been bruise marks that would have shown up at autopsy. So, the necklace was removed without making marks; not in a rush. If the killer had time to unclasp and remove the necklace, why not take the other jewelry? That undercut the theory that Brand had killed her in order to steal. Of course, it also weakened my theory about Park; unless he'd taken the necklace to make it *look* like a robbery to deflect suspicion. Nothing about the case was making sense.

I had a feeling that I was missing something; something I wouldn't find sitting behind my desk.

I decided to pay an unannounced visit to the Kellog place.

Eighteen

I drove across DC to the north loop of the Beltway, stopping in Silver Spring to grab a ham sandwich and cola for lunch, and then drove west to I-270 for the drive north to the Kellog place.

It was two when I arrived at the compound gate. Either the guard had been told that I was allowed unlimited entry, or my two visits had eased their mind about me. I got the same friendly smile and salute. I popped the hood and trunk and got out. While he did his inspection, no less thorough for my being familiar, I idly looked around.

On the top corner of the guardhouse roof, I noticed something I'd missed before; a cylinder mounted on brackets aimed down toward me. Peering closer, I saw the lens recessed in the cylinder. It was smaller than most video cameras, but unmistakable.

The guard had finished his inspection. He noticed where I was looking.

"Neat, ain't it," he said. "Latest technology; high definition, high resolution, multi-spectrum surveillance camera."

I get the high definition, high resolution part," I said. "But, what do you mean by multi-spectrum?"

"In addition to regular filming, it has the same shit as night vision goggles for night surveillance, and infra-red for fog or seeing a person moving through the trees. The focus can even be adjusted, so you see somebody, you can zoom in real close for an ID. Like I said, neat."

"That it is. You got these things all over?"

"Nah, just on the fence; we got the whole fence covered, looking out and about twenty to thirty yards in. Turk and Mr. Kellog figured if we had all the approaches covered, we didn't need a lot on the interior. Was me, I'd cover the house too, but I just work here, so nobody gives a shit about what I think."

"Where are they controlled and monitored from?"

"Well, we got control of the one on the

gate here in the guard house, and a small monitor we can switch from camera to camera to look over things. Turk's got a master monitor in the guard building, and Mr. Kellog's got a small master monitor in his office – in his desk I think. The two of them got control over all the cameras, and Mr. Kellog's got a recorder."

"He can record what all the cameras see?"

"Sure can. Turk says he keeps all the recordings in a computer file. I got no idea why; nobody's ever tried to break into this place."

"I'll bet that's because they see you dudes and that dog of yours, and decide it's not healthy."

He laughed. A little flattery is never out of place.

I got back in my car as the gate opened. Driving slowly toward the main house, I looked around, taking in my surroundings with an ultra-critical eye for the first time. Even from a distance, I could see the little boxes atop poles where the cameras were emplaced. I also noticed for the first time, the guard building, a low, one story white structure with a flat roof, off to the right and downhill from the main house. As I reached the point where the drive was closest to the building, the door in the center front opened.

Jennifer Kellog was instantly recognizable. She wore brown pants and a beige sweater that buttoned down the front. Even from the distance of about thirty yards, I could see that her hair was tousled and her face was red. She was frowning as she walked out the door. She was followed by Ted Wilson. He was dressed in his work pants, but only with a t-shirt that wasn't tucked in.

Wilson reached for her shoulder, but she shook it off and batted at his hand. She turned to face him, so I couldn't see if she was saying anything, and inside the car at the distance I was from them, could hear nothing. I did see, though, that he smiled and patted her cheek.

She whirled away from him and started toward the big house at a run. Wilson stood in the door watching her for a moment, then, smiling, turned and went back inside.

I arrived at the parking area just as Jennifer Kellog arrived at the front of the house. Her face was still red, and I noticed that the side zipper of her slacks was unfastened. There was a corner of a plastic bag sticking out of her front pants pocket. Her eyes went wide as she saw me getting out of the car, and she hesitated, as if unsure whether to greet me or flee.

"Is everything okay?" I asked as I

approached her.

"Uh, yes," she said. Her eyes flickered from side to side. She clasped her hands at her waist so tightly her knuckles whitened. "Why shouldn't things be okay?"

I stood in front of her, about three feet away. Not so close as to seem threatening, but close enough to be clearly in control. She didn't seem to notice, though, and her eyes didn't seem to be able to focus on me.

"You seem a bit upset, is all. I saw you at the guard office down the hill.

Her eyes widened momentarily, and she looked back down the hill.

"Has there been a security problem?" I asked.

"Security problem? Uh, no," she said. "I . . . I had a message for Ted, uh, Mr. Wilson."

It was a cool day, but there was a sheen of sweat on her forehead and little beads of perspiration on her upper lip. She hugged herself, looking at the ground in front of my feet. Not only was she nervous, but she was concealing something, and from the state of her hair and clothing, and the way Turk Wilson had been dressed, I could guess what it was. I wondered if Jackson Kellog knew that his security chief was shagging his only daughter right under his nose.

"I see," I said. "Must have been important for you to go all the way down there in person." Okay, I can be nasty sometimes. I was poking her in the eye. Poor little rich girl, having her way with the hired help. I didn't feel too much sympathy for her. "Anyway, I'm here to speak with your father about Penelope Laine's murder." Her eyes flickered faster. "Just thought you looked like you needed help."

"No, I don't need any help." A petulant tone had crept into her voice. "But, thanks for caring." That last was said without a hint of sincerity.

I stepped aside and let her proceed to the front door, following in her wake. She shrank back to avoid body contact when I passed her in the entrance foyer.

The Korean maid, Mary Lee, came into the area, glared at me, and gave Jennifer Kellog only a slightly less frosty look.

"Can you tell Mr. Kellog that I'd like to speak with him," I said to her.

Her head went back, and she gave me a look down the length of her not too long nose, and then spun on her heels and walked down the corridor toward Jackson Kellog's office.

She was back quickly, still looking as if I'd tracked dog poop in on my shoes.

"He say you come to his office," she said. Then, she turned and walked away; dismissing me without further ado.

Jennifer Kellog had made her getaway while I was distracted by the housekeeper. I was beginning to feel like an unwanted house guest the way the two of them were reacting to my presence.

When I entered Jackson Kellog's office, he was still behind his desk, but it had changed. The left pedestal was swung out, and atop it was a large-screen monitor with a complicated looking keyboard and a joystick control. The monitor was divided into four quadrants. The screen was blank.

"Ah, Mr. Pennyback," Kellog said. "I'm glad you're here." He was the first, other than the guard at the gate, who didn't seem displeased at my presence. "I was just about to call you. Pull that chair around here where you can see the screen; I have something to show you."

When I'd pulled the chair around, squeezing between his desk and the wall, he tapped the keyboard, and the screen came alive, with four different scenes showing. A few more keystrokes and there was just one picture on the screen. It was in color, a bit fuzzy, but clear enough to be able to recognize the different species of ornamental plants the camera was recording.

"Notice the time and date stamp at the bottom of the screen," he said. The date was the day of the murder, and the time was 18:15 in black scrolling letters. The time indicator changed each minute. Based on the use of the 24-hour clock system, I guessed that this was a system that had originally been designed for use by the military, and wondered how Kellog had gotten hold of it.

When the time indicator clicked at 18:20, a figure entered the scene. Upon closer view, I saw that it was Thomas Park. He was carrying a large pair of shears, with which he began trimming the ornamental plants. Kellog occasionally tapped a key, fast forwarding the picture by increments of ten to fifteen minutes. Park never left the camera's view. Finally, the time display read 20:15, and Park suddenly looked to his right. He stood, and, dropping the shears, began walking rapidly to his right until he was out of view of the camera.

There was no need for Kellog to explain it to me. Assuming the video file hadn't been somehow altered, here was photographic evidence exonerating Park. Part of me was disappointed; a good suspect eliminated; while another part was relieved, and if you'd put a gun to my head, I wouldn't have been able to explain my mixed emotions.

"Okay," I said. "That clears Park, but what about his wife. She'd be just as interested in protecting their secret, wouldn't she?"

"Yes," Kellog replied. "She would. But, during the time between Penelope's departure from the dining room and Joseph finding her dead, Mary was in and out of the room serving the meal. And, when Joseph and I came here to my office, she delivered freshly-made coffee. I don't see how she could have had time to go upstairs, commit a murder, and get cleaned up in order to serve us."

Of course. I hadn't ever seriously considered Lee as a suspect, for that very reason. As housekeeper, she was at the call of the family without much warning. Unless she was capable of super-human speed, which with her short legs, I doubted, getting from the kitchen to the upstairs, killing someone and stealing the necklace, then hiding it and removing any traces of the crime, would have been impossible.

"Right; so she's in the clear as well. What does that leave us with?"

He looked down at his gnarled fingers as they tapped the keys, shutting the equipment down.

"I hadn't really thought of that. I was just interested in proving to you that Thomas and Mary were innocent. I knew he was scheduled to work in that area somewhere, so I searched the stored recordings, and there he was. As strongly as Joseph feels about his friend, Mr. Brand, it appears that he's the only viable suspect left."

Not really, I thought, but that wasn't a discussion I was ready to have with him. I believed in Brand's innocence as much as he believed in the Koreans, and with them eliminated, the only viable suspects left were the members of the Kellog family themselves. I mentally eliminated Abigail Kellog. Her mental state was such, I doubted she'd be capable of maintaining concentration long enough to kill someone and then carefully remove a piece of jewelry, not to mention concealing the weapon and cleaning herself up afterwards. That left me, then, with four suspects: Jackson Kellog, his wife, Joseph, and Jennifer. I know; Joseph Kellog was my client, and why would the murderer hire a PI to prove another person's innocence? Damned if I know. All I do know is, people do strange things. The problem in his case was lack of motive. I'd have to have Heather see what she could find out about the relationship between Joseph and Penelope. Old man Kellog struck me as the cold and calculating type, perfectly capable of executing a crime like this; except that I figured he'd hire someone to do it for him. His wife, Mary Elizabeth, was something of a nonentity. She hadn't struck me as the independent-minded type. But, that could be a pretense. She'd have to go under the microscope again as well. That left, Jennifer Kellog. I was having a hard time putting a label on her. She seemed like the typical spoiled rich girl, accustomed to getting her own way, and probably bored out of her skull, but lacking the grit to do anything constructive about it. There was what was looking to me like an affair she was having with the hired help, but my guess was that was more out of boredom or youthful rebellion against her upright and uptight family, and Wilson was probably the one in control there. I suppose if Laine had discovered that, it was remotely possible she might kill to keep it secret. But, even as I thought it, I knew it sounded lame. My guess is, she didn't really give a damn, and probably wanted to get caught. Same thing for her coke habit, which the stay in a rehab center told me the family already knew about. I couldn't see any motive there.

Nineteen

There was nothing else for me to say to Jackson Kellog, so I thanked him for showing me the video and took my leave. As I approached the entrance foyer, I noticed directly ahead of me, the door to what I'd previously been told was the parlor was ajar. It had been closed when I arrived.

Quietly, I walked to the door and peered through the space between door edge and jamb. I couldn't see the whole room, but the end of the large mahogany coffee table that sat in front of a black leather sofa was in view.

On her knees at the edge of the table, Jennifer Kellog bent at the waist, dipping her head toward the table top, and the four lines of white powder neatly arranged there.

I watched as she sucked them one by one

into her nostrils, throwing her head back and sighing after each. When all that was left on the table was a few stray grains, she sat back, supported by her splayed hands, her legs straight out in front and her head back, looking up at the ceiling with a dreamy look on her narrow face.

At that moment, I think I could have walked in and picked her pockets and she wouldn't have noticed. She was in dreamland, in that place that addicts go when the substance they've injected, ingested, or snorted into their system starts to take effect.

I now knew one more thing for sure about Jennifer Kellog: she was definitely a cokehead. Cocaine can make a person do strange things, but I'd never heard of an addict becoming homicidal.

Twenty

The mind is strange in the way it works. As I started the Bug's engine, bits of disconnected thought and unrelated images flitted across my consciousness and coalesced into a coherent whole.

Image: Jennifer Kellog at the front door of the mansion with Ted Wilson, taking something from him and putting it into her pocket.

Image: Jennifer coming from Wilson's office, disheveled and upset, with the corner of a plastic storage bag sticking from her pants pocket.

Image: Jennifer sucking what had to be cocaine up her aquiline nose.

Conclusion: Wilson was supplying cocaine to feed Jennifer Kellog's addiction. She was probably paying for said supply with the world's oldest form of exchange; her sexual favors; and probably feeling used because of it. What if, my mind reasoned, Penelope Laine had tumbled to this little arrangement? Jackson Kellog didn't strike me as the type man who'd sit idly by while one of his underlings not only screwed his daughter, but screwed her mind up with drugs. If the old man found out, Wilson's job might not be the only thing he lost. Kellog had amply demonstrated what his wealth could achieve; he'd smuggled Park and his wife into the United States, out from under the noses of a military regime, and right under the noses of the world's greatest power. Arranging for Wilson to have a little 'accident' would be child's play for someone of Kellog's wealth.

I drove slowly down the drive until I was abreast of the guard office, and stopped the car. I got out and walked the few yards across the grass, and rapped on the door.

"Come in," Wilson's voice called.

Whatever I'd expected, Wilson's 'headquarters' wasn't it. The place was littered with papers, empty beer cans, and crusty pizza boxes all over the floor. The only neat place was the security camera monitoring station in the corner. Wilson sat sprawled on a ratty looking sofa, still in his t-shirt, and drinking vodka straight from the bottle. His eyes were bloodshot and teary.

"Well, Mr. Pennyback," he said, waving the vodka bottle at me. "To what do I owe the honor of this visit?"

I kicked a stack of greasy pizza boxes off a chair and sat.

"A few questions, if you're in any condition to even hear them."

His laugh was guttural.

"You criticizing my drinkin'?" he asked. "Hell, I'll have you know, I'm better drunk than most men are stone sober. What kinda questions you got?"

"Well, for starters; don't you think it's a bit stupid screwing the boss's daughter right under his nose?"

He was drunk, but no so drunk that my words didn't sink in. His face darkened, but his eyes widened.

"What gives you the idea I'd be doing anything like that?" He made an effort to sound belligerent, but it was weak.

"I don't miss much of what goes on around me," I said. "I've seen you two together, and it's clear that there's more than a casual relationship there. Question is, does Jackson Kellog know, and what might he do if he found out?"

His Adam's apple bobbed up and down, the half-empty bottle of vodka now forgotten.

"You plan on telling him?"

"Hey, she's legal age. What happens between consenting adults is none of my concern. I am concerned, though, about you supplying her with drugs. That *is* illegal. How long have you been doing it?"

"Whoa, pardner," he said. "You don't know what you're talking about."

He moved to stand, but teetered so badly, he fell back against the sofa cushion.

"I think I do, my friend. You're supplying her with cocaine. How long has that been going on?"

"That's none of your fucking business," he snarled. "You go to the old man with that story I'll rip your head off and shit down your fucking neck."

Spittle dribbled from the corners of his mouth. He pushed himself up from the sofa with some effort and turned to look down at me.

"Easy, friend; you're in no condition to tackle a one-armed cub scout. Right now, I've no intention of telling anyone anything. I'm just concerned that maybe, someone else – say, Penelope Laine – might have noticed the same things I noticed. If she did, she might be motivated to ingratiate herself with her new father-in-law, don't you think?"

He blinked, and looked at me, his expression completely befuddled.

"What the hell you getting at, dude?"

"That would be a powerful motive to kill her."

"Hold the fuck up, Jack," He said. "I didn't kill the Laine broad, and if you go around saying I did, I'll definitely kill *your* ass."

He drew his right fist back and swung, a roundhouse, which if he hadn't been so drunk, would have taken some effort to dodge, and would have done a hell lot of damage if not dodged. He *was* drunk, though, and telegraphed his swing like a Christmas letter. I leaned back in the chair, and brought my right foot up, the toe digging into his groin. He made an 'oomph' sound, followed by a high-pitched squeal as the pain signal from his mangled testicles reached his brain. As he doubled over, grabbing at his crotch, I stood, stepped to one side and brought the side of my hand down sharply against the base of his skull. He pitched forward, silent. He wasn't going anywhere for a few hours.

It's not right, I know, but hitting him felt good. It didn't totally balance the karmic scales, but it did tilt them a little back toward normal. I made a promise to myself to take that little quest up once I finished the job I was being paid to do.

I wiped my hand on my trouser leg and left the building.

Twenty-One

Joseph Kellog was waiting at my car, hopping from one foot to the other like he had a strong urge to go pee. He had a worried look on his face.

"I saw you stop," he said. "I need to talk to you."

"Talk," I said.

"Jennifer came to my office after you left. She said you saw her doing coke."

Damn, I thought; I would have thought she was too high to notice anything.

"Yes, as a matter of fact, I did. I also think she's been getting it from the chief of your security detail."

His eyes widened momentarily, and then

he shook his head.

"I can't say I'm surprised. I've always had my doubts about Wilson."

"Yet, you did nothing about it?"

He shrugged, and his face reddened.

"I . . . I . . . yeah, I suppose I should have done something," he said. "But, it's my fault she's using the stuff in the first place; so, if I go to dad with what she's doing, he'll find out, and . . . well, I've got a lot riding on not pissing him off right now. I mean, he knows she has a drug problem. We put her in rehab, and it looked like she was cured for a while. I guess she fell off the wagon."

Funny how it often comes down to selfish self-interest, which I suppose the rich have no monopoly on; it's just that, because they have so much they have more opportunities to be selfish pigs. Except for old man Kellog, and a lot of my feeling for him was based on the fact that he hadn't started out rich, I didn't see much to admire in any of this family. Two old women who were little more than ornaments, a spineless son, and a coke-snorting round heels for a daughter; the old man deserved better. The sooner I fingered the real killer and got Luther Brand off the hook, the sooner I'd no longer have to deal with this tribe of self-centered, spoiled pigs. I felt like rubbing Joseph Kellog's face in the dirt – literally, not metaphorically.

Instead, I brushed past him, got into my car, and drove back to Washington.

Twenty-Two

The next three days went by without much new happening – without anything happening in fact.

On Thursday morning, Heather was still busy researching, and I was sitting at my desk mentally reviewing our situation.

My mind was going around in circles; and getting nowhere. I knew the murderer had to be someone close to the family. I'd briefly considered Ted Wilson, but the crime scene photos I'd seen had convinced me that the murderer was someone known to Penny Laine. It was the only thing that explained the position of the body. It wasn't likely that she'd have been sitting if it was a stranger; and Wilson would have been a stranger.

That left the members of the Kellog family. Joseph was a remote possibility, but I couldn't think of a motive; same thing for Jennifer. Could the old man have killed his future daughter-in-law? I didn't want to go there; he was a self-made man who'd come from a background not dissimilar to my own. That didn't mean he wasn't capable of doing bad things, or breaking the law. He'd shown that when he sneaked two illegal aliens into the country. His motives for doing so were good, but it was nonetheless illegal. It didn't make sense that he'd kill Laine, but I couldn't dismiss it completely. But, if he'd done it or had it done, why? I'd ruled out Abigail, and didn't really see Mary Elizabeth Kellog as the type. So, there I was with three possible suspects, but without a convincing reason for the crime. A frustrating situation to be in; you know something must have happened, but you can't see a logical explanation for why; like a dream where you find yourself running toward something, but making no progress.

Worse, I was at a loss as to how I could possibly dig up a motive. Heather had dug into the family background to a fare-the-well, and so far had come up with zilch. Could it be, I thought, that I'd been wrong about Luther Brand? Had he been stupid enough to kill his friend's fiancée, who also happened to be his friend, according to him? All for a necklace that he'd have a devil of a time ditching? It made no sense. Nothing about this case was making sense.

Just as my mind was making the

umpteenth circuit around the endless loop that was leading me nowhere, Heather poked her head through the door.

"Hey, boss, got a minute? Got a couple of things I need to talk to you about."

I waved her in.

"I hope it's about this damn case," I said. "It's rapidly driving me crazy."

"Well, one thing is about the case," she said. "The other is personal. Which do you want first?"

"The personal's probably easy, so let's have it."

"You know next Tuesday's election day. I've volunteered to be an election monitor in my ward, so I'd like to take the day off."

I'd completely forgotten about the upcoming presidential elections. The incumbent vice president was competing with the governor of Texas for the top office in the land, and it had been a pretty nasty fight. The two men, both from political dynasties; the VP's father had been a long-serving senator, and the challenger was the son of a former president; were running pretty close in the polls. I don't normally follow politics, and frankly wasn't all that impressed with either of them, so the schedule had slipped my mind. Heather, though, can keep multiple trains of thought running smoothly in that mind of hers, and was a staunch supporter of the VP.

"Yeah, I guess that's okay. Now, what do you have on the case?"

"I've been running checks on all the Kellogs like you asked. Not a lot on the old man or the son, and nothing at all on Kellog's wife and sister. The two older women don't even leave the compound that often. But, Jennifer Kellog gets out quite a lot."

"Do her outings have anything to do with the case?"

"I don't know," she said. "I'll tell you, and you decide. I was running credit card charges against the family members, when I noticed a series of unusual charges on Jennifer's card just before it was cancelled."

"A rich girl like her had her credit card cancelled? I thought that only happened to poor people like us."

She opened her steno pad and flipped to a page upon which she'd written a column of dates and figures.

"Even the rich have limits," she said. "Look at this. She has more than twenty thousand a month in charges at this little casino in West Virginia over the past five months."

"Ah ha; so she must have exceeded the allowance daddy gives her, and couldn't pay her bill, so the company yanked her card. When was it cancelled?"

"About a month ago. You'd think she could go to her father for more money, wouldn't you?"

I told her about Jennifer's little chemical addiction, and her involvement with Wilson.

"She might worry that daddy might find out about her other habits," I said. "I get a sense that old man Kellog's not too sympathetic with weak people, and this girl's as weak as they come."

"So, what do you think?" she asked. "Is this information useful?"

"Could be. I'll need to check on her activities at the casino." I noted the name and address; not the big casino in Charlestown, but a smaller roadside place called 'Lucky Seven' located just over the Maryland state line on West Virginia Route 480. "Maybe I'll drive over there tomorrow and see what I can find out."

She snapped her notebook closed.

"You know, if you were really serious about me getting my license, you'd let me do that," she said.

"But, that would leave me here to answer the phones."

"So?"

Her face froze in a stubborn 'I'm not budging on this one' look. She had me on that, too. I'd been working with her for months so she could apply for a PI license, and if I wanted her to take me seriously, I would need to start letting her work in the field.

"Okay, I'll make you a deal," I said. "We'll both go, but I'll let you do the snooping and questioning, how's that sound?"

"Fair enough."

The broad smile that lit up her face, though, told me she thought it was a great idea.

Then, the phone rang. I knew it rang, because the little white light on my phone lit up, and I could hear a muted ring through the closed door. Heather looked at me, her eyebrows lifted. She stood there, like a blonde-topped ivory statue, a half smile on her face.

Dammit, I thought, I hate having to do stuff like this; that's why I hired her in the first place.

I picked up the phone.

"A.E. Pennyback, Confidential Enquiries," I said in my brightest voice. "How may we help you?"

"Is that you, Mr. Pennyback?" Joseph Kellog's voice asked. "What happened to your secretary?"

"Uh, she's not at her desk at the moment." Heather smiled and winked at me. "What can I do for you?"

"My father asked me to call you," he said. "He wanted me to deliver a message to you that he said you'd understand."

"Okay, shoot."

"He said that a plastic item from his extensive collection is missing. He doesn't know precisely when it went missing, but he does recall seeing it two weeks ago. Does that make any sense to you?"

It didn't – at first. Then, an image of Kellog's office popped into my mind. His extensive collection of plastic objects, ranging from a full-sized football to a miniature warrior's spear and shield. He'd had a little wooden rack on his desk containing a Lucite letter opener, but as I concentrated, I remembered that the rack had two sets of curved brackets. It was designed to hold more than the one letter opener he'd been playing with. My guess was, whatever was missing was probably shaped like a knife blade.

He'd known that when he was talking to me in his office, but had said nothing. Now, he was having the information passed to me by his son. What had changed? I had a feeling that I only had a little time to figure it out.

Twenty-Three

Sandra hadn't been pleased when I told I was going to a casino in West Virginia. Not because she's addicted to gambling, or even that she worried that I might see some eye candy among the women who frequent such places. No, she just wanted an excuse to get away from town for a while, but I didn't think putting the trip off until Saturday was a good idea.

When I told her I was taking Heather on her first field assignment, she eased off. Sandra and Heather are about as un-alike as two people can be; Sandra is tall and athletic, while Heather's head barely comes to my shoulder, and her idea of exercise is lifting her tea cup. The only similarities between the two of them are that they're both blonde, both beautiful, and both are devoted to me – but, for different reasons. I told her that the Lucky Seven, from what Heather had been able to learn, was something of a dive. Unlike the four main casinos in West Virginia, it had no hotel, no dog or horse track, and it didn't advertise. It was on a little back road, well off the beaten path, and frequented mainly by people who were referred to it by other people who were regular customers. It didn't seem like a place someone from Jennifer Kellog's social status would frequent, but there's no accounting for taste.

I got to the office earlier than usual on Friday morning, but Heather was there ahead of me. She was all decked out in a forest green safari suit, and had her blonde tresses pulled back into a bun; her idea of what the serious female private detective looked like. I was wearing brown chinos and a gray and blue Dallas Cowboys sweatshirt. She wore sensible brown loafers. I had on my crepe soled black hiking boots. I hoped the Lucky Seven didn't have a dress code.

We took my car, and drove north on I-270 to Frederick and then took U.S. 340 west to Charles Town. After we passed through Charles Town, we took West Virginia Route 9 north to Route 480 east back toward the Maryland state line.

We arrived around eleven. The casino, a sprawling, one-story building in the middle of a macadam parking lot filled with pickup trucks, semis, vans, and a few late model sedans, wasn't actually on Route 480, but off a one-lane paved road that angled off the main road, hidden from view until you were almost on top of it. The 'Lucky Seven' sign, a large neon monstrosity, over the main entrance, advertised it as a bar/restaurant. No mention was made of gaming of any kind.

I found a parking place in the back, and we walked back around to the front. Inside the entrance, it did look like a bar and restaurant, with a large open area for dancing and a stage off to the right. Two doors in the back of the room, at either end of the long bar, had large, beefy men standing near them. These, I figured, were the entrances to the gambling area, and one had to get past the golems at the doors in order to partake of the pleasures of the back room or rooms.

"Looks like getting into the casino part might not be as easy as I thought," I said.

Heather undid the top button of her safari suit jacket.

"Let me see if I can get us in, boss," she said, and with hips undulating, walked toward the nearest goon.

I followed close behind.

The guy at the door stood about six-four with shoulders that looked about four feet wide, thighs that bulged against his trouser legs, and the bulge of a nasty sidearm under the jacket that threatened to burst at the shoulder. He had a broad forehead and beetle brows, with a dark brown eyebrow that was one single line of hair above his bloodshot eyes. Those bloodshot eyes were focused on Heather's chest like sonar tracking an enemy submarine, and his fleshy lips were turned up in a smile.

"What can I do for you, sweet thing?" he asked, as Heather planted herself in front of him, craning her neck to look up at his face.

"My associate and I need to talk to the manager," she said.

Darned if she didn't sound like a real PI. I couldn't have done better myself. Actually, under the circumstances, I couldn't have done as well. I can't bat my eyelashes like Heather can, and I don't have a rack to display, at least not one that another man would want to ogle.

"Whaddya wanta talk to him about, darlin'?"

She reached up and put her hand on the lapel of his jacket, running her fingers up and down.

"I'm sure you'll understand, big fellow, that some things are confidential. This is a very sensitive matter that we can only discuss with the manager."

He was wavering. The big guy's body was quivering, and his ruddy face was getting darker. Little beads of sweat popped out on his upper lip.

"Uh, well, okay, I guess you can," he said. "Just turn right when you go in. You'll see the boss sittin' behind a window near the slots. You can't miss him."

"Thanks, big boy," she said in her best Mae West imitation. "I'll see you later."

His Adam's apple bobbed up and down so fast I was afraid the poor guy would choke to death. Heather brushed a finger across his chin and breezed past him. He didn't even notice me in her wake.

When the door had closed behind us, I laid a hand on her shoulder. She turned, looking up innocently at me.

"Where the hell did you learn to do that?" I asked.

"Oh, I saw it in a movie once. Did I do okay?"

"You did great, honeybunch," I said quietly. "Let's hope you can work your same magic on the manager."

The manager wasn't hard to find. There

was a booth projecting from the wall that had windows with little slots in them on three sides. A thin, bald man, impeccably dressed in a dark blue suit and string tie, sat on a stool inside the booth. His narrow eyes missed nothing as he scanned the room.

And, what a room it was.

About the same size as the outer room, it nonetheless was crammed full, with a three banks of a hundred-fifty slot machines to the right, blinking and humming as nearly that many people fed tokens in the slots and pressed the buttons to set the wheels spinning. To the front were several tables, alternating between Blackjack and poker, and on the left, a bank of TV monitors showing various sporting events. Elevated tables with stools lined in front of them were in front of the monitors, and a large crowd of mostly men perched on the stools, betting on the games being displayed. Several men in dark suits; clones of the two guarding the entrances, strolled about the space, keeping sharp eyes on the players, and ten waitresses dressed in low-cut faux bunny costumes flitted about the room with trays of drinks. The place hummed and clanged with excitement as gamblers vainly sought to beat the odds. Now and then, one of the slot machines lit up and played loud music as a lucky player hit one of the mini-jackpots.

The bald man missed nothing.

As we approached the booth, he pushed open the side and stepped out to face us.

He was only about a half an inch taller than Heather and looked to weigh about the same, but his expression was that of a man who was in complete command of his surroundings.

"You want to talk to me?" he asked.

The guard must have gone to a phone after we left and sent him a heads-up.

"Yes," Heather said. "We're working on a case in Maryland that involves a frequent customer of yours, and we'd like to ask you a few questions about her, if you don't mind. You're the manager, I take it?"

"Manager and owner," he said. "Name's Jake Logan; what can I do for you, sweetheart."

He appraised her with an appreciative glance, but frowned when he looked at me.

I took out my ID and held it up for him. He glanced at it, but his attention was on Heather. If he noticed that she didn't flash an ID, he wasn't indicating it.

"We don't normally talk about our . . . clients," he said. "People come here because they know we value their privacy."

"It really has nothing to do with what goes on here," Heather said brightly. "Look, this is a murder case, and we're trying to look at all possible motives. I can assure you, we're absolutely discrete."

He smiled, this time including me in its ambit.

"Well, well; I have to admit I've never encountered a private gumshoe who looks quite like you." He looked at me with a wolfish grin. "I guess you must be the muscle of the operation, and she's the brains, right?"

I saw no reason to contradict him, so I just nodded.

"Okay," he continued. "Who is the . . . client, and what do you want to know?"

"Is there some place we can talk a bit more privately?" Heather asked.

This seemed to impress him. Hell, it impressed me. She hadn't missed a beat so far.

"Sure, I have private office in the back. Come with me."

He turned and strode toward a row of doors to the rear of the slots. We followed.

His private office was small, but tastefully

furnished. A bank of TV monitors showing the various areas of the establishment sat in a large bookcase behind an ebony wooden desk. He sat himself in the large executive chair behind the desk and waved toward two high-back chairs in front of it.

"Okay, shoot," he said after we were seated.

"The client in question is Jennifer Kellog," Heather said. "Our information indicates that she's a frequent visitor."

His eyes didn't blink as he looked at her.

"Miss Kellog? Yeah, she comes in a couple times a week."

"What are her gambling preferences?"

He hesitated. I was afraid he'd refuse to talk, but then, he smiled.

"She plays the slots sometimes; only until a space at the one of the Blackjack tables opens up. She's a high roller; has a weakness for drawing cards when she's already close to busting."

"So," Heather said. "She's often a loser."

"Hey, it's hell to beat the house even if you're a good player, and our little Miss Kellog's not what you would call a good player. I think she just gets her kicks out of pushing it to the edge."

"She must drop a bundle every time she comes in," I interjected myself into the conversation.

The wolfish smile came back.

"This is getting into an area I'm not sure I should be talking about to you," he said.

"What you tell us stays between us," Heather said. "We're just trying to get a sense of her financial situation. It might be important to the case."

That seemed to placate him.

"Yeah, she drops at least twenty grand every visit; sometimes more. But, she's a rich girl, so I imagine it's not all that much to her."

There was some hesitation in his voice. I wasn't sure Heather had caught it, but she surprised me.

"You don't seem too sure of that," she said.

"Hey, you're a pretty sharp cookie," he said. "Okay, it's like this; she wasn't having any problems for a long time. She'd use her credit card to get cash advances, blow it, and after a few drinks, split. A few weeks ago, though, her card was declined. Man, was she pissed. Stormed out of here like a force five hurricane. Then, a couple days later she's back; only this time, she's flashing cash – must have been twenty, thirty grand – but, she blew the whole wad at the table."

"Had she come in with that much cash before?"

"Nah, she always used her card before. And, yeah, I was curious about that, too, so I asked her where she got so much money, figuring she'd hit her old man up for it. She got real nervous at first, but I pumped a few free drinks down her gullet, and she said she'd gotten it from Pearlie Mason."

"Who is Pearlie Mason," Heather asked.

His eyes narrowed. But, Heather just smiled and batted her lashes at him.

"Look, you sure this is just between us? I mean, Pearlie's a freelancer, but he's not somebody you want to cross, you dig."

Heather made a cross sign over her nearly exposed breasts, a view that wasn't lost Logan. The narrow-eyed look of suspicion was replaced by a wide-eyed expression of appreciation.

"I assure you, Mr. Logan; what you tell us is strictly private. Now, just who is Pearlie Mason?"

"Pearlie's sort of a pawn broker. He doesn't have a shop or anything. He just hangs around the restaurant area, looking for gamblers who've tapped out. I don't know who supplies him, but the guy's always flush with cash and for the proper collateral, he can refinance them."

"So," I said. "Jennifer Kellog got money from this Pearlie Mason character."

"Yeah, at least three times in the past two or three weeks. She never wears any fancy jewelry, so I don't know what she used for collateral, but she must have gotten over a hundred grand from him."

"Where can we find him?" I asked.

"He's probably in the restaurant," Logan said. "He holds court at a table by the entrance. You can't miss him. He's a ratty looking little dude who always wears brown."

We stood. Heather proffered a hand, which Logan took and held for a long moment.

"Thank you for your cooperation," she said. "You've been quite helpful."

"Always happy to help a pretty lady," he said. "You and your muscle here ever want to try your luck first few bets are on me."

She deftly extracted her hand from his

grasp, beaming at him.

"We'll keep that in mind," she said.

"Look, I know you plan to talk to Pearlie," he said, a worried look creasing his face. "Don't you be telling him I told you anything, you hear. I'd hate to have issues with him."

With all the muscle he had in the place, I found his fear of Mason strange.

"Not to worry," I said. "If he's looking for losers in need of money, we'll use that to approach him. He never needs to know we even talked to you."

"Just be careful. Word is Pearlie likes to cut people."

We thanked him, and left him sitting there watching Heather's rear as we walked out the door.

As we re-entered the restaurant, the heavy at the door leered at Heather.

"That was quick," he said. "You get what you came for."

Heather gave him a forlorn look.

"We did, but lady luck wasn't running our way today. Blew everything in just a few minutes."

I was getting more impressed with her by

the minute. She was almost as good as me at improvising.

"You quittin'?"

"Not much choice. We're tapped out."

He looked toward the entrance.

"Hey, you want to give it another go, there's a guy here who might be able to help you out."

"Unless he's a human ATM, I doubt he could help us," she said.

"Well, little lady, you and your friend here are in luck." He pointed to a small table just inside the door.

"See that dude over there?" A small, rat-faced man with lank brown hair that drooped over his ears, dressed in a loose fitting brown suit, sat at the table, a glass of beer cupped in his hands. "That's Pearlie Mason. You go talk to him; he can help out for sure." He laughed. "Human ATM; that's cute. And, that's just what he is."

The rat-faced man looked up, a noncommittal expression on his face, as we approached the table.

"The man at the door said you might be able to help us out," Heather said.

The noncommittal expression quickly

morphed into a slightly greedy leer.

"Depends on what kinda help you need," he said.

"My, uh, boyfriend and I made a few stupid bets at blackjack and lost our money," Heather said. "That man said you make loans."

The slightly greedy leer got distinctly greedy.

"Well, hon, he was right. Pearlie Mason at your service. Pull up a chair and let's talk."

I noticed that he favored his right hand as he fondled the beer glass, so I sat in the chair to his right. Heather took the chair on the left. He didn't look dangerous, but I haven't survived as long as I have by underestimating people. A scorpion's small, too, but if you don't pay attention, its sting can be fatal.

"Now," he said. "How much you be needin'?"

I decided that it was time to take charge. This one seemed immune to Heather's charms. The only thing that seemed to interest him was the prospect of getting two more suckers in his clutches.

"Well, it's not exactly money we need," I said. "What we need is information about a friend of ours. I understand she's done some business with you."

He tensed; his attention focused on me. His hands moved away from the beer class toward the edge of the table.

"I ain't in the information business, friend," he said coldly. "Maybe you and the chippie better move on."

I leaned forward, putting my hands on the table.

"Before you do something we might both regret," I said. "It might be better if you hear me out. You loaned money to a woman named Jennifer Kellog, and I just want to know what she used as collateral."

"Dammit, fella, you must be hard of hearin'. I said scram."

His right hand started moving off the edge of the table. When it was halfway off, I reached over and clamped my left hand around his wrist, squeezing. His eyes screwed up in pain.

"Aw, damn, you breakin' my wrist you fucker."

Heather watched it with eyes wide.

"I'm not breaking it yet," I said. "But, if you don't start answering my questions within the next few seconds, I will." I exerted a bit more pressure, drawing tears from his eyes.

"Okay, okay," he said, trying to hold back the tears. "So, I let the Kellog bitch have some bread. So what?"

"How much, and what did she use for collateral?"

He grunted in pain. I squeezed again to remind him that there could be more pain.

"Hey, okay, let up. She hit up for just over a hundred grand. She used jewelry, diamonds; pretty classy stuff, I thought."

"What kind of jewelry?"

"First two times, it was a bracelet and earrings. Stuff fetched a good price up in New York. Last time, she brought me this necklace had a rock in it the size of your fist. But, the bitch stiffed me. I took it up to New York, and my . . . the dealer what looked at it said the rock wasn't a real diamond. It wasn't worth more'n two hundred bucks. Bitch never showed up again, but if she does, I'm gonna cut her cheatin' heart out."

I eased up on his wrist, and had him describe the necklace. His description, rough as it was, coincided with the description of the necklace Penelope Laine had been given by Mary Elizabeth Kellog – except for the bit about the diamond being fake. I asked him what he'd done with it.

"Shit, I took the two C notes the buyer offered. No sense in the deal bein' a total loss. That chick's got a gambling jones real bad; I figure she'll be back here any day now, and when she shows up, me and her gonna have a nice private chat."

I didn't bother telling him that I didn't think Jennifer Kellog would be coming back to the Lucky Seven. Her luck had just about run out.

I knew now who had killed Penelope Laine. I couldn't even tell myself why I knew it; I just knew it. Now, all I had to do was prove it.

Twenty-Four

It was late afternoon by the time Heather and I got back to the office. We spent the remainder of the day writing up our notes. I also told her that she'd done a good job her first time in the field, and that we'd be applying for her PI license the following week – after the elections.

To say that she was elated would be a gross understatement. She almost choked me with the big hug she gave me.

"I've been waiting for that for a long time," she said. "That was a real high, being in the field, although I don't think I'll ever be able to handle people like Pearlie Mason like you did."

"Well, you can just keep being the brains, and I'll supply the muscle," I said.

We both laughed.

"So," she said. "We know Jennifer Kellog has a gambling addiction in addition to her drug addiction, and we know she's in to a loan shark for a lot of money. Where does that get us?"

"Well, for one thing, it tells me who must be Penelope Laine's killer. Of course, there's just one little hitch; I can't prove a damn thing."

She looked at me, all innocent with those baby blues of hers, like she had no idea what I was talking about.

"How could going to that dump of a casino, and talking to those two terrible men tell you the name of the murderer? I mean . . . oh . . . you don't mean . . . you think Jennifer Kellog killed her?"

"Either that, or she had Wilson, the guard chief, do it for her," I said. "At least that's the way the evidence is pointing."

"What evidence?"

I laid it out for her. Jennifer's drug habit and her gambling addiction; her affair with Wilson; and now, her money problems, and how she'd solved them, all added up to a lot she might want to hide. If Laine had somehow found out any of it, it could just have spooked her, or Wilson – or both of them – enough that they'd want to shut her up. Taking just the necklace, which turned out to be worthless anyway, would have successfully diverted attention away from them and toward robbery as a motive if they'd thought of taking some of the other valuables.

It was all so clear in my mind. But, it was also all circumstantial, more so even than my theory on Brand's innocence. If I was going to nail them, I'd need something more solid. But, it was late on a Friday; Sandra was waiting at home for an account of my visit to Babylon; her name for the casino; and a gourmet meal just waiting for me to cook it. I'm only human. I was looking forward to the weekend and an opportunity to purge my mind temporarily of the doings of the Kellog clan.

I caught most of the rush hour traffic on the way home, so it was after six when I pulled into my front yard. Sandra was sitting on the couch listening to the radio, a glass of white wine in her hand, when I walked in.

"Hey, babe," she said. "I figured you'd be a bit late, so I started without you."

I leaned over and kissed her on the forehead.

"Let me take a shower and grab a beer, and I'll join you."

A hot shower and a change into brown chinos and a long-sleeved polo shirt, I padded barefoot first to the kitchen where I grabbed a cold bottle of *dos equis* beer, and then I joined her on the sofa. Beethoven's *Ninth* was being played by the Philadelphia Symphony Orchestra. I let the warm sounds and rhythms of the strings sooth me as I sipped the cold beer. Just as the sounds caressed my ears, the smooth, slightly bitter liquid massaged my taste buds. Sandra leaned against my shoulder, adding the comforting warmth of her body heat to the mix.

When the last strains of the music had faded, we went into the kitchen and prepared supper together, me doing breaded pork chops, okra, and corn bread, while Sandra did a tossed salad made of spinach, iceberg lettuce, chopped walnuts and diced apple, with a vinaigrette dressing. She had another glass of white wine with her food, while I washed mine down with another beer.

After supper we listened to some old radio shows on the NPR station. Sandra chided me about not getting a television, but I reminded her that it would be a wasted expense and would take up space in the room for nothing. We both agreed that there little on TV worth watching; even the news broadcasts had turned into overly made-up performers vying for ratings instead of journalists providing information about world events. So, with no TV, and little else on the radio that caught our interest, we showered together, which was thirty minutes of raucous fun and a water-soaked bathroom, and then crawled into bed.

We didn't get to sleep for several hours, and slept in on Saturday morning.

Our weekend was relaxing. Runs in the woods, beating hell out of the heavy bag in the barn, showering and horsing around, light meals that, thanks to balmy November weather, we ate on the back porch, where we enjoyed the view of the forest taking on its fall colors; the reds and golds, the yellows and oranges, overlaying the stubborn greens. We watched the leaves as they one by one gave up their precarious perches and drifted lazily to the earth which was covered with grass that was already beginning to turn yellow.

When I drove into the office Monday morning, I was still feeling giddy from my restful weekend. Heather's smile when I walked through the door, told me she was still high from her first foray into the field.

I was feeling optimistic. Nothing could bring me down.

"Hey, kid," I said. "You want to leave early today, so you can get ready to do your election judge thing tomorrow?"

"Yeah, that would be nice. I just read the letter they sent me. They want us to be at the polling station at 5:30 in the morning."

"Yikes. That's an ungodly hour to start anything."

"Well, they say the polls have to open at 7:30, and people start lining up by 6:00. We have to get everything ready, or there'll be pandemonium. Don't you like to vote early?"

I hadn't thought about it, really. I vote in national elections every four years. I don't bother with the oddball elections for the House of Representatives every two years, and couldn't tell you the name of my county elected officials, but I do feel an obligation to vote for the president.

"Heck, kid," I said. "If you're out all day, there's hardly any reason for me to come into the office. I'll probably go by my polling place around 8:00 or 8:30, on my way in here. Doubt if there'll be much for me to do."

"Answer the phone and take notes," she said. "I'll sort it out when I come in on Wednesday."

The phone on her desk rang.

"A.E. Pennyback, confidential enquiries, how may I assist you?" she said slowly and precisely. I knew this was more for my benefit that the caller. She was telling me how she wanted me to answer the phone while she was out.

Her eyes widened and two spots of color appeared in her cheeks.

"Oh, I see," she said. "Do you want to speak to him? Okay, hold on."

She pressed the 'hold' button and looked up at me with a sad expression.

"It's Joseph Kellog," she said. "You'd better take it in your office. There's been another murder at the Kellog place."

As I started for my office, I heard her telling Kellog I was just about to pick up.

I snatched the phone from its cradle.

"Yeah, Al Pennyback here," I barked. "What's this about another murder?"

"Uh, it was . . . is, Turk," he said. "Ted Wilson, the head of security."

To say I was shocked at the news would be something of an understatement.

"What happened?"

"I don't know. One of the guards found him yesterday afternoon in the guard building. He'd been stabbed in the chest."

"Any leads as to who did it?"

"The police came. They're not saying much," he said. "But, I did overhear the woman who does the technical stuff say that it looked like he'd been stabbed with a weapon similar to the one used to kill Penny."

"Let me guess; no signs of struggle, or the presence of anyone else in the room."

"That's right. How did you know that?"

"Just lucky," I said. "Look, I'm coming out to your place. I need to talk to everyone there. Have the police left?"

"Yes, they took lots of photographs and then took the body and left. They think maybe he might have had a tiff with one of the guards, but they can't pinpoint anyone."

"Okay, let the guards know I'm coming. I imagine they're a bit trigger happy right now."

I rang off and told Heather where I was going.

"Be careful, boss," she said. "That place doesn't seem too healthy right now."

Twenty-Five

I drove five miles per hour over the limit most of the way, only slowing down when I hit the little road to the compound gate.

A new guy was at the gate. He didn't look happy or friendly when he waved me to a stop. I rolled down the window.

"ID, please," he said, holding a hand out.

I passed my ID to him.

"I'm expected," I said. "I'm working for Joseph Kellog."

He looked at my ID, then at a clipboard he was holding. Then, he looked down at me, still unsmiling.

"Okay, Mr. Pennyback, you're on the list. Please step out of the car."

His tone was all business. Unlike the almost friendly tone I'd received at my last visit. I popped trunk and hood and got out.

His partner, a guard I'd seen in the booth on my first visit, came out of the guard shack with a mean looking Doberman on a leash. The dog gave me a mean look, but responded to a not so gentle tug on the leash and went for my car. While the second guard did a 360 external check, with the dog sniffing as he peered under the carriage with a mirror on the end of a long pole, the first guard stood near me, his hands on his hips, but with the right hand not too far from the 9 mm Sig Sauer on his hip. The atmosphere was tense and frosty. I decided to try and warm it up a few degrees.

"Sorry to hear about your boss," I said. "Happened yesterday some time, did it?"

He continued to stare frostily at me. The guard inspecting my car, though, stopped and looked at me. There was a guarded, but not unfriendly, look in his eyes.

"Yeah," he said finally. "He was supposed to do the rounds at five, and when he didn't show up, one of the guys went up to check. Found him sittin' on the couch. Somebody had stabbed him in the chest."

"Any idea who? Did the guys on the gate see anyone near the building?"

"Nah, not a clue," he said. "And, you can't

see the front of the building from down here, so no, they didn't see anybody. Of course, they're paid to watch for threats from the outside, so they wouldn't have been lookin' up that way in the first place."

Of course, I thought. They probably wouldn't think of anything bad coming from inside the compound, even after Laine's death. These guys were well-trained; probably too well-trained. They would do what they were trained to do, and little else.

"You think there'd be any objections to my taking a look at the scene? I mean, the cops have finished with it, right?"

"No skin off my nose. With Turk gone, I'm not even sure if we'll still have jobs. This outfit was a one-man show. Turk gave the orders and we carried them out. I reckon old man Kellog's the one to ask."

"Thanks, I'll do that."

He'd finished inspecting the Bug, which was as clean as could be. He then ran a metal detector wand over me from head to foot, and let the dog have a sniff at me. Satisfied that I was no threat, he motioned toward the house.

"You know where to park," he said, as he headed back to the guard shack.

The gate began silently opening as I got

back behind the wheel.

I parked on the visitor's pad and walked to the front door. The Korean housekeeper, still frowning at me with her lips curled in distaste, opened the door. A nervous-looking Joseph Kellog stood behind her.

"Come on in, Mr. Pennyback," he said. "Father's waiting for you in his office."

I followed him down the hallway. The housekeeper followed close behind. Jackson Kellog was sitting on the sofa across the room from his desk. He looked up as I entered.

"Mr. Pennyback, please have a seat." He motioned to the arm chair to his right. "Mary, please bring us a pot of coffee. I assume coffee will be fine with you?"

I nodded.

Joseph sat on the sofa next to his father.

The old man's face was creased with worry. He'd aged ten years since I last saw him, and he didn't seem interested in playing his power games at the moment.

I decided to get right to business.

"Do the police have any ideas as to who killed Wilson?" I asked.

"If they do, they're not sharing it with us," he said. "It's really quite frustrating. Two murders right here in my home."

He was a man accustomed to being in control, and having his way. His actions in getting the two Koreans into the country were evidence of that. I could almost sympathize with him; the case – now, cases – were frustrating me, but, for a different reason. He seemed to be frustrated at not being able to determine the outcome of events; I was frustrated because I knew the killer's identity, but hadn't been able to find the facts that would enable me to disclose it.

"Mr. Kellog, I'd like to talk to certain members of the family again. But, before I do, I'd like your permission to take a look at the new crime scene."

He looked startled at first.

"Why on earth would you want to do that? The police have already gone over it with a fine-tooth comb. Besides, we haven't had a chance to clean it up yet. It's really quite gruesome."

"The police look for physical evidence; fingerprints, strands of hair, and stuff like that," I said. "I try to get an emotional sense of the scene. It's not very scientific, but I've found that observing the scene gives me mental impressions that the police often miss. As to gruesomeness, I've seen more than my share of blood and gore, so that's no problem."

That's as close as I can come to telling people that I often get visions of what happened when I'm at the scene of a crime. I'm no psychic, but my mind works that way sometimes. It's as if the victims and perpetrators leave invisible traces of their anguish that my mind is able to detect. Sometimes, it only comes to me later in dreams – dreams that often feature my late wife, Sarah. I know it makes no sense, which is why I keep it to myself. I've never even told Heather or Sandra.

"Well," he said. "I don't suppose it can do any harm. You know how to get there. The door's not locked."

"Thanks. I'll be back here in half an hour. I'd like to talk to your wife first, if you don't mind."

His expression said, 'whatever for?', but he kept his mouth closed. He merely nodded.

"Do you want me to come with you?" Joseph asked.

"No; I think it would be better if I went alone."

I didn't want his presence cluttering up my observations.

Mary Lee came back with a silver urn on a

silver tray, surrounded by silver cream and sugar containers and three expensive-looking china cups and saucers. As I squeezed past her, she gave me a look that I couldn't interpret.

Twenty-Six

When I arrived at the guard office and opened the door it hit me right away. Death, especially violent death, has a unique set of odors. There's the metallic smell of blood, the rank odor of voided bowels and bladder, and the sour smell of fear and despair that hangs over the scene like a storm cloud. The place looked as untidy as it had when I'd visited before, with the addition of a dark blotch on the sofa and the floor where Ted Wilson's life blood had gushed from his body and pooled into a blackish-red gelatinous mess.

I stood in front of the sofa and let my mind drift, trying to get a mental image of what had happened. From the shape and disposition of the blood stain on the sofa, he had been sitting when he was stabbed. There was only minimal disturbance of the outlines of the stain – no real movement of his body, indicating he'd been killed quickly, and in all likelihood by someone he knew well enough to allow up close. Jennifer Kellog fit that description, but I doubt the police had even looked her way. Just as I was sure they hadn't considered her, or any other member of the Kellog family, in Laine's murder.

No matter how long I looked, though, I couldn't get a clear mental image. In my mind there was a fuzzy picture of Jennifer Kellog, but it wasn't clear enough to give me a hint to motive and exactly how she'd done it.

I fished around in my pocket until I found the name card the crime scene investigator Susan Dickey had given me. I took out my cell phone and dialed her number.

"Lieutenant Dickey," her bright voice said. "How can I help you?"

"Lieutenant, it's Al Pennyback. You got time to answer a few questions for me?"

"Oh, Al; do call me Susan," she said. "I'm a bit disappointed that you didn't drop in to see me. But, of course I have time for you."

"Uh, well, yeah, sorry I haven't come by. Been awful busy with my case and now of course, there's the second murder here."

"Yeah, Ted Wilson, the chief of security," she said. "That's kind of got us busy here as well. What is it you want to know?"

"For starters, I'm told you guys think the same weapon was used to kill both Wilson and Laine; is that right?"

"Not precisely. The entry angle on Wilson was different for one thing. Laine was stabbed directly from the front. Wilson's wound entered at a slight angle from his right. But, the size, shape and depth are consistent with the same or a very similar weapon being used."

"So, you're operating on the assumption that the same person killed them both?" I know that at this point I would.

Her tinkling laugh came over the line.

"Look, tall, dark and handsome, I just assess the evidence for the investigating detective; in this case O'Malley. It's up to him to draw conclusions, and he hasn't shared them with me."

There was more meaning in her words than might at first be intuited. I detected some bad blood between her and O'Malley.

"I know that, but you're as intelligent as you are beautiful." No harm in using a little flattery. "Surely you have your own ideas about what the evidence means."

"Sure, big boy," she said. "Just between you, me and the gate post, I think it was the same perp."

"Is O'Malley still fixating on Luther Brand?"

"I don't know, but if he is, he's ignoring a significant piece of evidence."

"Which is?"

"Luther Brand has a tracking device affixed to his ankle," she said. "If he gets more than a hundred yards from his bungalow, or tries to take it off or disable it, it sounds an alarm here. It hasn't sounded the alarm since we put it on him. And, this is the real salient fact: the current crime scene is nearly two hundred yards from his place. No way could he have done it."

Well, at least one part of the Washington County Sheriff's Department was on my side. That still didn't give me the concrete facts I needed to nail the real murderer, but it made me feel better.

"One more question, Susan," I said, placing emphasis on her name. "When you guys took the call for the Laine murder, did you search the entire house looking for the murder weapon?"

"No, we didn't. We tossed the room she was found in, checked every knife or cutting implement in the kitchen, and of course, did a thorough search of Luther Brand's bungalow."

"It didn't occur to you that the weapon might have been hidden somewhere else in the house?"

"Hey, babe, O'Malley was in charge. I just searched where he said search." There was a pause. "Look, you gotta remember, we're dealing with Jackson Kellog here. He's not exactly small potatoes in the county. You don't lightly do things that cast aspersions on people like him. Besides, when we tumbled to Brand's record, and O'Malley focused on him as a prime suspect, it didn't seem necessary. You aren't saying you think one of the Kellogs did it, are you?"

I didn't want to cause her any problems, and I still didn't have enough to go around spouting off.

"I'm not saying anything – yet. I just believe in checking out *all* possibilities."

"That's because you're not a public official, dependent upon the goodwill of the citizenry; especially the well-heeled citizenry, Al, dearest. Look, when this is all over, any chance you might call me?"

"And, why I never will be a public official," I said.

I said I'd call her again when I had time – a slight, white lie, because I had no intention of contacting her when this case was done – and rang off.

Twenty-Seven

Mary Elizabeth Kellog was waiting for me when I got back to her husband's office. She was sitting beside him on the sofa, clasping one of his hands with both of hers and looking like a condemned prisoner awaiting execution.

"She's a bit nervous; this second murder got to her," Kellog said. "Do you mind if I sit in while you talk to her, for moral support?"

I did mind, but it didn't seem to make sense to alienate him at this point. He'd be pissed enough when he found out that I was looking at his baby girl as a cold-blooded, cold-hearted killer.

"No," I said. "In fact, I can talk to the both of you at the same time, get it all over with."

That seemed to please him a bit, but he still had a sad cast in his eyes.

"Thank you." He patted her hands. "Don't worry, dear. Mr. Pennyback seems to know exactly what he's doing. Just answer his questions as truthfully as you can."

She nodded. Her eyes glistened.

"Ok-kay," she said. "What d-do you w-want to know?"

"Tell me about the jewelry you own," I said.

Her eyes went wide; so did Jackson Kellog's.

"What does her jewelry have to do with the murders?" he asked.

"Bear with me. The cops say that the motive for Penelope Laine's murder was the theft of a rather expensive necklace. I'm just trying to fully understand the case, and tie up all loose ends."

"Well, I have a rather extensive collection of jewelry, mostly diamonds." As she talked about her jewelry, she relaxed and her face became more animated. "I have a few items that Jackson gave me over the years, but most of my jewels were passed down through my family from mother to daughter, beginning with my grandmother.

She ran her fingers over the necklace she was wearing, a small oval diamond in a simple setting on a plain gold chain.

"My grandparents came to this country from Rhodesia in 1910; it was a British colony at the time. Grandpa owned a farm in the southeast part of the colony. One of his workers found diamonds on the land; they were almost just lying on top of the ground." She turned to her husband. "What is it they call them, Jackson, dear?"

"Alluvial diamonds, Mary Elizabeth," he said.

"Yes, alluvial diamonds. Anyway, I'm afraid dear grandpa was a better farmer than businessman. He went into the diamond business with some shady characters, and in a few years had not only lost most of the money from the diamonds, but his land as well. He and Nana, my grandma, took what little they had left and came to America. Of course, what they had left was the diamonds that he'd had made into jewelry for her, and among them was a necklace made from that first diamond; a five-carat stone he'd had cut in an oval and set in a nice filigree gold setting. There were also several pairs of earrings, four other necklaces, and about half a dozen bracelets. A small fortune really, but they wouldn't part with it. They've been passed down from mother to daughter ever since. I plan to give them to Jennifer if she ever . . . uh, when she gets married. But, Joseph was so happy with poor Penelope, I thought it would be a nice wedding gift for her."

"Have you ever had your jewels appraised, Mrs. Kellog?" I asked.

"Well, yes, when we insured them, but that was years ago."

"Do you have any special security for them? I mean, they must be worth quite a lot now?"

"No, we don't," she said. "I keep them in a jewelry box in my bedroom closet."

"We have top security on this compound," Jackson Kellog said. "There's no way a burglar could get in."

Unless, I thought, the burglar just happens to already live inside the compound. There was no way a murderer could get in, either. I didn't say this, though. How do you tell someone their daughter is not only a murderer, but a thief?

I could do her a favor, though.

"Mrs. Kellog, you might want to have all your jewelry appraised again, just to be on the safe side."

I noticed that Jackson Kellog stiffened at that. Out of the corner of my eye, I saw that his skin was pale, and he was looking thoughtful.

Twenty-Eight

I had no further questions for Mrs. Kellog, but I did have a couple of bones to pick with her husband. She seemed grateful when I thanked her and told her she could go. Jackson Kellog, though, gave me a hard look when I asked him to remain.

"What more do you want from me?" he asked.

The steel I'd heard in his voice when we first met was gone. The old man sounded tired.

"One thing I'd really like to know," I said. "Is why you waited so long to tell me about the missing letter opener?"

"I, uh, told you almost as soon as I discovered it."

He tried staring me down, trying to look

me directly in the eyes, but his eyes kept flickering slightly to the right. I looked back at him, unblinking. We held gazes locked like that for several seconds. I had the advantage, of course. In the first place, he was lying, and in the second, I'm able to go for up to two minutes without blinking; I often do when I'm meditating. My internal clock told me we were at the forty-second mark when he blinked. He looked away.

"Now, Mr. Kellog," I said gently. "You and I both know that's not true. When did you first notice the item missing?"

When he turned back to look at me, I saw the misery in his rheumy eyes.

"How did you know?" he asked simply.

"It's a talent I have. I always know when people are lying to me. What I don't know, though, is why you're doing it?"

He was backed into a corner, but he wasn't ready to give up yet. His nostrils flared.

"That's of no consequence at the moment," he said. "Yes, you're right; I did notice the letter opener missing earlier. I didn't think it was important at first; hardly actually noticed it was missing. More of a feeling, you understand. I mean, I have so many plastic geegaws here, who'd notice one out of place? Anyway, the more I thought about what the police had said about how poor Penelope was killed; I guess my subconscious was working; the more I came to realize that the missing letter opener fit the description they had of the possible weapon."

"Do you know when it went missing?"

"I'm not sure. I seem to remember using it the day before the murder; but I can't swear to that. My best guess is that it was removed around that time, though."

I mentally reviewed what each family member had told me about his or her movements on the evening Penelope Laine was killed. A few more pieces of the puzzle fell into place. I began to see the path I needed to follow to reach the end of my quest.

"Thanks for finally being straight with me," I said. "Now, I think I need to talk to Jennifer."

"She's usually sitting on one of the side porches this time of day," he said. "Or, would you prefer I sent for her so you could talk to her in here?"

"No, I'll go to her."

"Why do you want to talk to her?" His worried look deepened. "She's already told the police and you that she didn't see anything the night Penelope was killed, and I doubt she knows anything about Wilson's death."

"Just routine," I said. "She might have noticed something that didn't seem important at the time. I just like to cover all bases."

That seemed to placate him, but only a bit. He still had that worried look.

Twenty-Nine

When I left the room, Jackson Kellog was sitting on the sofa, his shoulders slumped. He was a man defeated. He knew that I knew. What's more, I was convinced that he'd come to the same conclusion himself at some point. The question in my mind was, why he'd let things go on as long as he had. Unless he decided to come clean, though, I'd probably never know.

As I pulled the door shut behind me, I turned right, about to head to the door at the end of the hall that led out onto the porch, when I saw Thomas Park and Mary Lee come around the corner from the foyer. He had a determined look on his face. She looked like she would have preferred being anywhere else but where she was; in front of him as he not-so-gently guided her toward me.

"Mr. Pennyback." He pronounced it 'Pennybacku', which actually didn't sound too bad. "I must talk to you. *We* must talk to you."

"Is it important?" I asked.

"Yes, very important. But, we not talk here." He motioned toward the porch. "There be better."

I turned back toward the porch. They followed behind me, their feet making scuffing sounds on the carpeted hallway. The door to the porch wasn't locked, and the porch was unoccupied. A rattan sofa and two chairs sat in the center of the space around a glass-top rattan table. I walked over and sat on one of the chairs. The two Koreans took the sofa. Park sat with his shoulder against his wife's. She kept her gaze fixed on her hands which were folded in her lap.

"Okay," I said. "What's so important that it couldn't wait?"

He said something to her in rapid-fire Korean. She responded in kind. The language was full of harsh gutturals and sounds like throat clearing. I didn't understand the words, but it was clear that he was urging her to do something, and she didn't want to do it.

They went back and forth, both faces getting red, and the volume of their voices rising, but he seemed to be winning. Finally, she seemed to deflate, and glared at me. He laid a hand softly on her shoulder.

"Tell him," he said.

"Okay, I tell him," she said, but she didn't seem too happy to comply. "Yesterday, just before I hear about that Mr. Wilson found dead, I was setting table in dining room. I saw Miss Jennifer come in front door. She look very upset, and her clothing is messy. She not see me, but I see her go upstair."

One more piece of the puzzle, albeit small, clicked onto the board. Chances were Jennifer was coming from the guard building. It would give me a small edge when I talked to her.

"Was she carrying anything?" I asked.

"I didn't see. She hurry upstair. I don't think anything of it at time."

If she'd been carrying a bloody, Lucite dagger, it would have been the all-important corner piece that stays hidden as you try to get the sky done in a jigsaw puzzle without having the picture on the box as a guide. I didn't have the picture on the box, but I had the advantage of knowing things that she wouldn't think I would know. The question; was it enough?

"Thank you for telling me this," I said. "I think I must go and talk to Ms. Kellog now."

Thirty

I retraced my steps back down the hall, and crossed the living room to the curved staircase leading up to the second floor.

At the top of the stairs I came to a short hallway that ran from the front of the house to a cross-hallway. A set of double doors to my left front led, I knew, to the master bedroom, and to my right, I saw the door to the bedroom I'd been told was Jennifer's. I walked to the right and then turned left. In front of me was a door leading out onto the balcony.

Jennifer Kellog, dressed in a beige blouse that was semi-transparent and showing that her small breasts were not encased in a bra, and matching voluminous pants, sat at a round table near the railing. Her slender feet, with bright-red nail polish on her toes, were bare and propped up on an adjacent chair. Her narrow face was framed by her hair, which was combed straight and tight against her skull. As I approached, she wiped at her nose, which was red as if she had a cold. She made a sniffing noise, and looked up at me.

"So, now it's my time for the third degree is it?" Her speech was slightly slurred.

I noticed a minute trace of white powder above her upper lip, and there were traces of powder on the glass top of the table. She'd just been snorting. This could get tricky. I don't have a lot of experience talking to junkies, but the few times I've encountered them have been frustrating. I would have to proceed slowly and carefully, so that her coke-fogged brain could keep up.

"That only happens in the movies," I said.

I sat in the chair across the table from her and leaned forward, keeping my expression neutral.

"I just need to ask you a few questions," I continued. "Just to try and get events clear in my mind."

She leaned back in the chair, looking at me down the length of her aquiline nose. Her eyes seemed to have trouble focusing.

"I've already told you all I know about Penny's death."

"It's not just that I want to talk to you about. First, I'd like to talk to you about Ted Wilson."

Two bright blossoms of red appeared on her cheeks. Her eyes glistened.

"T-that was terrible what happened to Ted," she said, her voice quivering. "But, I don't know anything about it. I was up here most of the day."

High as she was, she was still a consummate actress. The way her eyes, as unfocused as they were, darted from side to side, I could tell she was lying.

"You and he were close, weren't you?"

She put a hand to her breast.

"Close? What do you mean by that?"

I leaned forward and placed my hands flat on the table.

"Close as in lovers," I said.

There was a sharp intake of breath. The spots on her cheeks got darker.

"How dare you!" She was trying for

righteous indignation, and falling short. "What on earth leads you to think such a thing? Ted worked for my father."

"The one thing has nothing to do with the other . . . at least, I don't think it does. As to why; let's just say I'm observant. I saw the way you two interacted with each other." Then I dropped the bomb. "That, and I saw you coming from his office the other day, and your condition was . . . let's say, a bit disheveled."

She shrank inside her clothes. It had been a wild shot, but it had hit home. But, it had only disconcerted her for a few seconds.

"Okay, so I was screwing him. How is that any business of yours?"

She did a bit better at a belligerent attitude. Of course, a poor little rich girl like her probably had a lot of practice at being belligerent.

"If that was all it was, it probably wouldn't mean anything," I said. "But, he was also your supplier."

Her eyes widened.

"S-supplier? Supplier of what?"

This girl had a repertoire that a Broadway performer would have died for. She'd gone from belligerent to feigned innocence without missing a beat. But, I wasn't buying.

"Come on, Jennifer; let's not play games with each other. I recognize the signs of a coke addict; you might as well wear a big sign around your neck. And, the day I saw you coming from his place, I saw the plastic bag of coke in your pocket. What's more, I saw you snorting it in the little room near the entrance as I was leaving."

She looked at me intently. Her panoply of feigned expressions had been put away. Now, she stared at me with cold malice in her eyes.

"Not much gets past you, does it? I saw you peeking around the door that day. You're not as quiet as you think, buster. Okay, so I do a few lines of blow now and then, so what? And, what if Ted provided it to me? He's dead now, so you can't do anything to him about it."

Now, it was time to take the gloves off and play hard ball.

"I'm not a narc, sweetheart," I said. "If you want to suck that shit up your nose, that's between you and the local authorities. I'm interested in something else entirely. How did you pay him for the drugs? Even if he was madly in love with you, with the street prices of coke, I can't see him doing it for free."

She smiled; a cold, mirthless expression.

"Let's just say we traded one commodity for another."

I didn't need for her to go into details. The state of her clothing the day I saw here told me what commodity she brought to the trade.

"A symbiotic relationship, eh? Sounds to me like he was important to you."

"You could say that. It meant I didn't have to hang around the streets or other places to get what I need, and it was a diversion. Not much else to do around this fucking place."

"So, tell me; why did you kill him?"

She wasn't expecting that. Her face paled, and she stopped breathing for a moment.

"I d-didn't kill him . . . w-why would I want to do that?"

"That's what I was hoping you'd tell me. You were seen coming from the direction of his office shortly before his body was found. Can you explain that? Did he threaten to cut off your supply?"

She stared at me; her effort to control her emotions was visible in the way the muscles in her cheeks twitched. I sensed that anger was just below the surface, and if I could get her mad, she'd become rash and careless – at least, that was my hope.

"Or, maybe the commodity you were supplying was no longer enough. What happened, he get too kinky for you?"

"Hah! Kinky? Ted wasn't very imaginative in that department. The occasional BJ was about as kinky as he ever got. He preferred the missionary position. Boring, but it got me what I wanted." I should have been shocked at language like that coming from someone who was supposed to be from the more refined class of people. Somewhere along the way this girl had dipped into the gutter, and seemed to thrive there. But, she was getting angry, though. Her cheeks were flaming again. "No, the dirty bastard got greedy, that's what. Decided he wanted money *and* sex in exchange for my coke."

She put her hands in the pockets of her trousers, and blazed defiance at me with her eyes.

"That's why you killed him?"

"We had a deal, and the fucker tried to change the terms. I argued with him; tried to tell him I didn't have enough cash right now. He grabbed me by the throat and started choking me, and threatening to rat me out to the cops. I stabbed him to keep him from killing me."

The actress was back. She seemed to actually believe the yarn she was spinning;

not enough to keep her eyes from flickering, but her voice was level as she spoke.

"So, he attacked you, and you killed him in self-defense. Why didn't you tell the cops that? I'm sure they would have understood."

"Are you kidding? Then, I'd have to explain why I was there in the first place. I-I guess I just panicked. So, when the cops came, I just kept my mouth shut. I told them I'd been in my room the whole time. They didn't ask me too many questions anyway."

"There was no report of drugs found in the office when the police investigated. What'd you do, take what he had left?"

"Why not; he had no more use for it, now did he?"

"What did you do with the knife you stabbed him with?"

Her body tensed.

"Uh, I don't remember. I just panicked. I must have dropped it on the grounds somewhere. Look, if you tell any of this to my father, or the cops, I'll just deny it. It'll be your word against mine."

Her smile was almost triumphant. She thought she had me in a corner. She was right, though; with just that, I didn't have much chance of making O'Malley, or any other cop, believe me. A black private investigator from DC's word against a rich white girl whose father's the richest man around; hell, I probably wouldn't believe me.

I needed to push her harder.

"Was it the same blade you used to kill Penelope?"

Her face fell momentarily, but she made an effort at recovery.

"No . . . I mean, I didn't kill Penny."

Now was time to drop the dime.

"Oh, I think you did, I just don't know why. I also think you did it with the plastic paperweight you took from your father's office."

Her eyes went wide. She stood up, her body tense. Her hands were still in her pockets as she moved around the table toward me.

"You think you know everything, don't you? Well, you don't know anything, and you can't prove anything." Tears were flowing now, but they were tears of anger, not sadness. "Penny had it coming. If she'd only listened to me, but no, she had to be Miss Goody Two-Shoes. She was going to tell my mother the diamond in her necklace was fake. I couldn't have that. I tried to reason with the bitch, but she just wouldn't listen. The self-righteous bitch thought I'd agree with her that telling mother was the right thing to do. My mother would have had puppies if she'd found out I've been sneaking her precious diamonds out and replacing them with zirconium. Shit, she values those stones more than she does me."

Then, the last piece of the puzzle fell into place. Penelope Laine, an experienced jewelry buyer, had recognized that the 'expensive' necklace she'd been given as a wedding present was paste. Her essential honesty compelled her to tell Mrs. Kellog, but she'd probably confided first in Jennifer, not suspecting that the rock was fake because Jennifer had replaced it to pay for her gambling. Of all the motives for murder, this is the lowest.

"Thanks for admitting it." Her eyes widened further. "Not to worry, I'm not wired or anything, but when I tell the police that you're guilty of not one, but two murders, and what you used, it'll just be a matter of time before they find it. Then, young lady, you're toast."

Her whole expression changed. Her face contorted like a cubist painting, and her body quivered. She lurched toward me, her right hand coming out of her pants' pocket. I caught a glimpse of the glint of light off the piece of plastic she was clutching, a clear plastic replica of a dagger. She brought it up and jabbed it at my chest.

"You'll never get to tell them, you son of a bitch," she screamed as the dagger came closer.

I'd been sitting relaxed, or that's what it would have looked like to her. But, I'm never totally relaxed when I'm in the presence of a potential killer. I reached over her oncoming hand and clasped her wrist with my right hand, and rapped her hard on the chin with the knuckles of my left. Her head snapped back, and her body went limp. The knife clattered to the floor. I grabbed her by the shoulders and gently slid her down to the floor. I pulled my handkerchief from my pocket and picked the knife up; careful to only touch the hilt so I wouldn't smear her prints. I was pretty sure that a careful examination of the blade, despite her efforts to clean it, would reveal traces of blood in the tiny imperfections in the plastic.

I then took out my cell phone and dialed Brian O'Malley's number.

Thirty-One

O'Malley and his crew of county sheriff's deputies broke speed records getting from Hagerstown to the Kellog compound. Jennifer was still dazed when they arrived, but when O'Malley saw the knife, and confronted her with it, she caved and began ranting and screaming.

They had to call a county ambulance and take her away under guard and in restraints.

To his credit, O'Malley went personally to Luther Brand's bungalow to remove the tracking device. I spoke briefly with Joseph Kellog, and told him the advance he'd paid me had covered my expenses and fee, and I'd be refunding the balance. He told me to forget it. He seemed in a daze.

The whole Kellog household – minus Jennifer, who was throwing tantrums as they loaded her into the ambulance - was in a daze when I left, heading home. Old man Kellog couldn't meet my eyes, and his wife had retreated to her bedroom. It had been a hell of a way to start the week.

I called Heather and told her I'd be going home rather than coming back to the office, and suggested she close up and go home. I promised to fully brief her on Wednesday, because I'd decided not to even open shop the next day. I declared an election-day holiday.

Sandra took one look at the expression on my face when I walked through the door, and silently went to the kitchen and got me a cold bottle of beer. She sat next to me on the sofa, massaging my shoulders as I knocked it back in three gulps. When I'd finished it, I went out and got another, pouring her a glass of white wine as well.

We ate supper in silence, and at around ten, crawled into bed. I pulled her close, burying my nose in her hair. I didn't yet feel like talking, and she respected my need for silence. That's why I love her.

The next morning, she ate a quick toast and coffee breakfast and went off to Takoma

Park to vote in the ward where she's registered. At nine, I drove to the Potomac Recreation Center on Falls Road. There was a long line, but things went smoothly, and I'd voted and was on my way back home by eleven, arriving just ahead of Sandra. She didn't ask me who I'd voted for, and I had no need to ask her. She wore her politics on her sleeve, and would never think of voting for a republican. I hadn't been following the election news that much, but finally cast my vote for the vice president. I've never trusted Texas politicians. Since Montgomery County, Maryland is staunchly democratic, I just voted for all the other democratic candidates. No sense wasting my vote.

I was stirring up a pot of chili when she walked in.

"Smells good," she said. "And, I'm starved."

"Why don't you whip up a salad, and I'll make corn bread. It's pretty nice out, so we can eat on the back porch."

"Sounds great. First, though, I need to take a shower."

After her shower, the lilac scent of her soap competed with the heady aroma of my chili – her lilac won. We ate in silence at the little wooden table I bought at a swap meet for my porch, sitting on two plastic chairs I picked up at the local Wal-Mart store for three bucks each.

The chili bowls had been sopped clean with the last bits of corn bread, and we were sitting there, enjoying our second beers and watching a herd of deer graze at the edge of the wood line.

"You ready to talk about the case now?" she asked.

I was. It was like opening a dam that water's built up behind. It came gushing out in a torrent.

I told her about Penelope Laine, a woman I'd never met, but someone I think I would have liked. A woman who'd made her own way in the world, and finally met someone who loved her unconditionally, and was prepared to give her a life that most middle class people can only imagine. A woman who believed in doing the right thing, and the right thing would have been to tell Mary Elizabeth Kellog that her prize necklace wasn't what she thought it to be. Her belief in doing the right thing had gotten her killed. The crime scene photo, taken just before they removed her body, showed a gentle looking young woman, her expression placid even in death, with a large flower-shaped red stain on her white satin dress from the roundness of her breasts down to the lap.

And then, there was Jennifer Kellog. Born to privilege, she should have had everything going for herself. She was a person who'd never had to want for any of the physical comforts of life. What she'd missed, though, were the important moral and emotional values that make a person worth something. She had many paths available to her, unlike many of us, but she'd chosen all the wrong ones, and for all the wrong reasons. I was convinced that both murders had been planned and coldly executed. That she'd stolen the blade and had it with her when she encountered both victims indicated premeditation.

I'd solved the case, and given Luther Brand back his freedom, but it gave me little satisfaction. Maybe it's my middle class upbringing, or the values I picked up in the army, but I think the scales should always be balanced. Those who do wrong should pay for their wrongdoing in some way equivalent to the wrong they've done. I'm not big on the death penalty as a punishment, because it's irrevocable. If you make a mistake and execute the wrong person, you can't say 'oops' and make things right. But, life in prison, in some hell hole of a jail somewhere, seems appropriate for someone who has deprived another of life. It was unlikely, though, that Jennifer Kellog would end up doing hard time in a real prison. Her father's money would get her a platoon of high-powered lawyers who would argue diminished capacity, or some other socially acceptable explanation for why people kill, and she'd be confined to a mental institution. And, again, I'd bet anything that her father's wealth would ensure she was assigned to a top-notch institution.

The real crime was, I didn't think she was insane. Crazy, without a doubt; you have to be a little crazy to stick a blade in someone's chest, but not medically insane. As I looked back on our encounter, I realized that she was playing me. She knew the jig was up, and was setting me up so that my testimony would support an insanity defense. After all, why else would she try to kill me as well, if she wasn't wacko?

But, that's the way the system works in this country. If you can afford it, you get a defense that covers all the bases, and makes sure you get every advantage the law allows. Someone like Luther Brand, on the other hand, would be assigned an over-worked public defender who, while probably capable, just wouldn't have the resources or time to look for all the legal loopholes on his client's behalf.

It wasn't fair, but there wasn't a damn thing I could do about it. I should have to be content with having kept an innocent man out of jail. That wasn't a completely bad feeling; just not as complete as it could have been.

The scales of justice were out of balance. In this case, the blindfold over justice's eyes weren't ensuring impartiality; they were obscuring the facts. Jennifer Kellog wouldn't be judged by a jury of her peers any more than Luther Brand would have been. In his case, the twelve good citizens would have been from a world he'd never inhabited. The same could be said for Jennifer. It was unlikely that the county would summon twelve millionaires to sit on the jury at her trial, if the case ever even went that far. No, her expensive lawyers would get together with the prosecutors in a little room somewhere in the government offices and wangle a deal. Hell, with her old man's money, she was unlikely to even spend more than a night in lockup.

It wasn't fair. But, life's like that. It's hardly ever fair; especially when it comes to the select few who occupy the top of the economic ladder. I'm no avenging angel, but it pisses me off to think about justice being perverted that way. One set of rules for the rich, another for the rest of us.

I was also disappointed in Jackson Kellog. His sense of loyalty to family and friends was a kind of perversion as well. He had to know that his daughter was the killer. He knew about her drug addiction, and in hindsight, I didn't see how he could have been unaware of her gambling and the assignations with Wilson. He hadn't risen to the top of his industry by being stupid and unobservant. He might have come from a humble background, but being rich had warped his mind. Maybe he just wanted to protect his daughter, but to do so at the expense of others, people he might have considered somehow inferior, was why I feel the way I do about the super-rich.

That's the way it is, though. The rich just aren't like the rest of us. They live in a parallel, but completely different world.

Books by this author:

Al Pennyback mysteries

Color Me Dead
Memorial to the Dead
Deadline
Dead, White, and Blue
A Good Day to Die
The Day the Music Died
Die, Sinner
Deadly Intentions
Death by Design
Till Death Do Us Part
Deadly Dose
Dead Man's Cove
Dead Men Don't Answer
Deadly Paradise
Kiss of Death
Death in White Satin

The Buffalo Soldier series:

Buffalo Soldier: Trial by Fire
Buffalo Soldier: Homecoming
Buffalo Soldier: Incident at Cactus Junction
Buffalo Soldier: Peacekeepers
Buffalo Soldier: Renegade
Buffalo Soldier: Escort Duty

Other fiction

Angel on His Shoulder
She's No Angel
Child of the Flame
Pip's Revenge
Wallace in Underland
Further Adventures of Wallace in Underland
Dead Letter and Other Tales
The White Dragons
The Dragon's Lair
The Last Gunfighters

Nonfiction

Things I Learned from My Grandmother About Leadership and Life
Taking Charge: Effective Leadership for the Twenty-first Century
Grab the Brass ring
African Places: A Photographic Journey Through Zimbabwe and southern Africa

About the Author

Charles Ray has been writing fiction since his teens. He won a Sunday school magazine writing contest when he was thirteen, and having his byline on a short story published in a national publication forever hooked him on writing. During his time in the army (1962-1982) he often moonlighted as a newspaper or magazine journalist, and was the editorial cartoonist for the Spring Lake (NC) News, a weekly newspaper, during the 1970s. In addition to his writing, he was an artist/cartoonist and photographer for a number of publications, including Ebony, Eagle and Swan, and Essence, and had a monthly cartoon feature and did several covers for Buffalo, a now-defunct magazine that was dedicated to showcasing the contributions of African-Americans to the country's military history.

After retiring from the army, he joined the U.S. Foreign Service, and served as a diplomat in posts in Asia and Africa until his retirement in 2012. He has worked and traveled throughout the world (Antarctica is the only continent he hasn't visited), and now, as a full time writer, continues to globetrot looking for interesting things to write about, draw, or take pictures of.

A native of Texas, he now calls Maryland

home. For more on his writing and other projects, check one of the following Web sites:

http://redroom.com/member/charles-a-ray
http://charlesaray.blogspot.com
http://charlieray45.wordpress.com
http://www.twitter.com/charlieray45
http://www.facebook.com/charlieray45
http://www.flickr.com/photos/charlesray45/
http://www.viewbug.com/member/charlesray

www.ingramcontent.com/pod-product-compliance
Lightning Source LLC
Chambersburg PA
CBHW072203170626
46813CB00003B/771